Tales of Fearful Forests and Wicked Woods

Short Stories of what Lurks in the Deep Dark Places

British Library Cataloguing-in-Publication Data
A catalogue record for this book is available from
the British Library

Contents

Selected Biographies of the Authors

The Boy and the Wolves, or The Broken Promise

ANDREW LANG

Once upon a time an Indian hunter built himself a house in the middle of a great forest, far away from all his tribe; for his heart was gentle and kind; and he was weary of the treachery and cruel deeds of those who had been his friends. So he left them, and took his wife and three children, and they journeyed on until they found a spot near to a clear stream, where they began to cut down trees, and to make ready their wigwam. For many years they lived peacefully and happily in this sheltered place, never leaving it except to hunt the wild animals, which served them both for food and clothes. At last, however, the strong man felt sick, and before long he knew he must die.

So he gathered his family round him, and said his last words to them. 'You, my wife, the companion of my days, will follow me ere many moons have waned to the island of the blest. But for you, O my children, whose lives are but newly begun, the wickedness, unkindness, and ingratitude from which I fled are before you. Yet I shall go hence in peace, my children, if you will promise always to love each other, and never to forsake your youngest brother.'

'Never!' they replied, holding out their hands. And the hunter died content.

Scarcely eight moons had passed when, just as he had said, the wife went forth, and followed her husband; but before leaving her children she bade the two elder ones think of their promise never to forget the younger, for he was a child, and weak. And while the snow lay thick upon the ground, they tended him and cherished him; but when the earth showed green again, the heart of the young man stirred within him, and he longed to see the wigwams in the village where his father's youth was spent.

Therefore he opened all his heart to his sister, who answered: 'My brother, I understand your longing for our fellow-men, whom here we cannot see. But remember our father's words. Shall we not seek our own pleasures, and forget the little one?'

1

But he would not listen, and, making no reply, he took his bow and arrows and left the hut. The snows fell and melted, yet he never returned; and at last the heart of the girl grew cold and hard, and her little boy became a burden in her eyes, till one day she spoke thus to him: 'See, there is food for many days to come. Stay here within the shelter of the hut. I go to seek our brother, and when I have found him I shall return hither.'

But when, after hard journeying, she reached the village where her brother dwelt, and saw that he had a wife and was happy, and when she, too, was sought by a young brave, then she also forgot the boy alone in the forest, and thought only of her husband.

Now, soon the little boy had eaten all the food which his sister had left him, so he went out into the woods, and gathered berries and roots, and while the sun shone he was contented and had his fill. But when the snows began and the wind howled, then his stomach felt empty and his limbs cold, and he hid in trees all the night, and only crept out to eat what the wolves had left behind. And by-and-by, having no other friends, he sought their company, and sat by while they devoured their prey, and they grew to know him, and gave him food. And without them he would have died, in the snow.

But at last the snows melted, and the ice upon the great lake, and as the wolves went down to the shore, the boy went after them. And it happened one day that his big brother was fishing in his canoe near the shore, and he heard the voice of a child singing in the Indian tone, 'My brother, my brother! I am becoming a wolf, I am becoming a wolf!'

And when he had so sung he howled as wolves howl.

Then the heart of the elder sunk, and he hastened towards him, crying, 'Brother, little brother, come to me'; but he, being half a wolf, only continued his song. And the louder the elder called him, 'Brother, little brother, come to me', the swifter he fled after his brothers the wolves, and the heavier grew his skin; till, with a long howl, he vanished into the depths of the forest.

So, with sorrow and anguish in his soul, the elder brother went back to his village, and, with his sister, mourned the little boy and the broken promise till the end of his life.

The midnight embrace
Matthew Lewis

Albert, lord of the ancient castle of Werdendorff, on the borders of the Black Forest, was a nobleman of elegant person, and fascinating manners; but his heart was prone to deceit. He was well versed in all the wily arts of seduction, and he paid slight attention to the fulfilling of either religious or moral duties, when opposed as a bar to his pleasures.

At the distance of half a league from his stately abode, resided the fair Josephine in an humble cottage, happy, virtuous, and respected. Beauty and innocence were the only dower she possessed. Her father had been a subaltern officer in the emperor's service. Her mother was the only child of a very poor, but very respectable pastor. Francisco, her father, had fallen in the field of battle when she had attained her fifth year. His disconsolate widow retired with her trifling pension from Vienna, where she had hitherto resided, to the vicinity of Werdendorff, where she lived with her darling child in a peaceful and retired seclusion now so congenial to their feelings. The education of Josephine she attended to with the most sedulous care, and was amply repaid by the docility of her pupil. At the age of sixteen, Josephine lost her parent, who, previous to her dissolution, gave every advice that a virtuous mind could dictate, with regard to the subsequent conduct of her daughter. Josephine listened to her virtuous counsels with attention, and while the pearly drops chased each other down her pallid cheeks, promised a strict adherence to the wishes of the dying parent. Alas! how little to be depended upon are the promises and resolutions of mortals!

The remains of the mother of Josephine being decently interred, the sorrowing girl soon felt herself obliged to grant less indulgence to heartfelt grief, that she might toil for each day's bread. Her parent's pension expired with her; and our fair maid, to pay the rent of her cottage, and defray her necessary expenditures, was obliged to leave her humble pallet with the first salute of the lark, and ply her needle with assiduous and unremitting industry. Her labour was crowned with success. She lived happy, virtuous, and respected, for the first three years after her mother's decease. She was then predestined to experience a fatal reverse: the veil of innocent simplicity was to be torn from her mind, and the vacancy filled up by the dark cloud of guilt.

Albert of Werdendorff beheld the maid in all her native pride of beauty, softened by angelic modesty, and her unconsciousness of the superlative charms she possessed. Albert longed to call this fair floweret his own; not as a tender

4

admirer, to protect her honourably from all the storms of fate, but as a rude spoiler, that wantonly plucks the rose from its native branch, and then, regardless of its beauties, casts it to wither on the ground.

It is needless to describe minutely the various arts that Lord Albert descended to, in order to seduce the unsuspecting victim of his deceptions. His superior rank, fortune, and connections were so many circumstances to furnish him with favourable pretexts to forward his designs.

Though Albert was lord of the castle of Werdendorff, and had there a splendid establishment, yet he depended on his father for a princely addition to his possessions. He made Josephine to believe that it was impossible for him to espouse her during his father's life; but called on heaven, and every saint, to witness the inviolable faith and constancy he would always maintain towards her: that he should always regard her as his wife; and, as soon as he should be free to offer his hand, their marriage should be legally solemnized. Josephine had many virtuous sentiments; but Albert, by sophistry, overcame those scruples; and the unfortunate maiden added one more to the many that suffer their credulous hearts to be seduced by the wily serpent, like objects of their tender and faithful love.

Josephine's breast was no longer the abode of serenity. In Albert's presence her spirits were elated; she listened with delight to the repetition of his vows, and blinded by delusive passion, esteemed herself one of the happiest of the happy. But in the lone hours of solitude, she was oft times miserable. Regret, remorse, and apprehension, would enter, though obtrusive guests. From the casement of her cottage, Josephine could behold the stately castle of Werdendorff, and discern its portals opened for the reception of guests invited to the noble banquets and festive balls, which often made its lofty roofs resound with their mirth. On these occasions Josephine would sigh, and ponder on the wide difference between herself and

Lord Albert in their stations, and wonder if her fond hopes would ever be realized.

At midnight, when all the inhabitants of the castle were wrapt in repose, was the time that Lord Albert paid his visits to Josephine's cottage, which hour was mutually chosen by the lovers for their interviews, that they might elude the observation of those around them. And when the moon gave no ray of light to Lord Albert in his progress over the dark and fenny moor, Josephine would place a lighted taper at her casement, to guide him to her humble abode.

Ah! ill-fated maid! thou didst soon experience the dire truth, that men betray, and that vows can be broken; and that illicit love, though at first ardent, will soon decay, and leave nought but wretchedness behind.

Albert had been Josephine's favoured lover about six months, when, one hapless night, Josephine had placed the taper in her window as usual; and sat wishing the arrival of Albert in anxious expectation. More than once she conjectured she heard his well-known footsteps approach the door. She flew to open it, and her eye fixed on vacancy alone, while she shed bitter tears at the disappointment. Another, and another night elapsed; Albert came not; and Josephine's anguish and suspense became insupportable.

On the fourth morning of Albert's unusual absence, Josephine arose from her pallet after a few hours of restless and perturbed sleep; she approached the window, and her eyes taking their usual direction across the moor to the castle of Werdendorff, she beheld its gay banners streaming on the walls.

Anxious to learn the cause of this rejoicing, Josephine mingled with a group of rustic maidens who were repairing to the castle. She asked them, in tremulous accents, what propitious event they were celebrating at the Chateau; but the villagers were as ignorant as herself. When they came to the outer portal of the edifice, they beheld a gay procession passing from the hall to the chapel.

The sentinel, in reply to Josephine's interrogatories, informed her that Lord Albert was then gone to the chapel to seal his nuptial vows with Lady Guimilda, the proud daughter of a neighbouring baron, whose possessions were immense, and she the sole heiress.

Josephine replied not; her heart was full, even to bursting. She retreated from her companions, and seeking the covert of a friendly wood, gave way to all her frantic ravings of despair, which was still aggravated by every passing gale, bearing along the echoes of the loud shouts of revelry that pervaded the castle, and proclaimed Albert's perjury and her ruin.

As soon as the first violence of her grief was abated, she began to cherish delusive ideas. She thought the sentinel might have deceived her; or, at least, he might have been in an error himself, in supposing Lord Albert the bridegroom of the proud Guimilda; and she thought it more probable that it was some friend of his, who had solemnized his marriage at Werdendorff castle.

Cherishing this weak hope, she returned to her cottage; and partially disguising herself in a long mantle, and a thick white veil, she repaired at twilight to the castle, and, unobserved, mingled in the revelling crowd. But alas! the sentinel's intelligence she soon found to be too true; and the gayest among the gay throng was the false Albert and his bride Guimilda.

Once convinced, Josephine tarried no longer in the castle-hall. With torturing sensations, and faltering steps, she left the abode of her haughty rival, and once more sought her lonely dwelling. The night was dark, and the wind shook the rushes, and all around, like her own heart, was drear and forlorn. With folded arms, and her whole person like the statue of despair, sat Josephine by the casement. Fond recollections caused her tears to flow, when she called to mind how oft in that window she had placed the taper to light her then ardent lover over the moor.

While she was thus reflecting, she heard footsteps approach her cottage door; and presently she heard her own name softly pronounced. She instantly recognized Lord Albert's voice; and opening the casement, she cried indignantly, 'Away to Guimilda! Away to the pleasures that reign in Werdendorff castle. Why leave you my rival's bed, to add another insult to the woes you have caused me?'

Lord Albert renewed his entreaties for admission; and Josephine, at length, imprudently yielded to his request.

Albert exerted all his eloquence to convince the fair one, that his heart had no share in the nuptial contract with Guimilda; that there Josephine's image reigned triumphant, while her rival could claim nought but his hand. By the stern command of his father, he protested he had joined his fate to Guimilda's, who would only leave him his fortune on that condition: but that his love to Josephine should never be diminished by that circumstance; but that he would transplant her to a more pleasing abode, where she might reside in elegant retirement, and appear in a situation more congenial to his wishes than her present dwelling would allow, or, indeed, her near vicinity to the castle render prudent.

The soft blandishments of her deceiver again lured her to guile; and her anger was completely vanquished by love.

Again was the board spread with the choice delicacies, and delicious wines, that Lord Albert had brought with him from the castle; the flower-footed hours winged away with rapturous delight, and again the soft smile beamed on the lovely countenance of Josephine.

'Adieu, my beloved,' said Lord Albert; 'the first blush of morn empurples the east, and warns me from thy arms.'

Josephine inquired affectionately when she was next to

expect her loved lord. He replied, that he would return at the *dark hour of midnight*, and again clasp her in his arms.

Lord Albert's bosom beat high as he sped homewards across the moor. The horrid deed he had committed, did not at that moment appall him. He congratulated himself on being freed from a mistress, whom satiety had for some time past made him detest.

In relating to Josephine the cause of his marriage with the Lady Guimilda, he had been guilty of a great falsehood. The known wealth of the heiress, at first, induced Lord Albert to visit at her father's villa; for avarice was a ruling passion with the youth. But when he beheld the haughty fair one, he instantly became a captive to her beauty, and loathed Josephine.

His nightly visits to Josephine, though conducted with much cautious secrecy, had by some means reached the ears of the proud Guimilda. No pity for the poor maiden filled her breast; she hated her fair rival, for having a prior claim to Lord Albert's heart. Her revengeful temper made her feel that she should never enjoy perfect happiness while Josephine existed. She thought that there was more than a probability, that, for all Albert's declarations to the contrary, when she conversed with him on the subject, that, after a short time would elapse, his heart might grow cold towards the legal partner of his fortune, and return with redoubled ardour to his deserted mistress. She knew the infirmities of her own temper; and the angelic sweetness of disposition which her informants had represented Josephine to possess, contrasted with her own hauteur, caprice, and tyranny, made the confirmation of her fears appear as strong as proofs of holy writ.

To glut her revenge, and leave no room for apprehension, she formed the horrid project of demanding the following sacrifice at the hands of Lord Albert.

This was the removal of Josephine by a poison which should

take a quick effect, and cause her to breathe her last ere she
should have time to reveal the name of her murderer. The time
fixed on by Guimilda for the perpetration of this horrid deed,
was their wedding night. Albert was to make some plausible
excuse to his guests, to account for his absenting himself at that
time, and then to repair to Josephine's cottage; and, as he
always, on those occasions, condescended to convey with his
own hands, some refreshments, it would be an easy matter for
him to infuse into the goblet of wine that he should present to
his fair victim, a deadly but tasteless drug that Guimilda prepared for that fatal purpose. The proud Guimilda made a
solemn vow, never to admit Lord Albert to her bed, till her
horrific demand was complied with.

Alas! her destined husband was too pliantly moulded to her
purpose; he made not half the resistance she expected to en-
counter; but, after a very few scruples, signified his perfect
acquiescence with the will of this fiend in female form.

How Lord Albert effected his purpose has been previously
described. He had nearly gained the castle on his return, when
his own words recurred to his memory: at the dark hour of
midnight he would again return, and clasp her in his arms. 'Ill-
fated Josephine!' exclaimed he, mentally. 'Ere that hour
arrives, thy fluttering breath will flee amid agonizing pain;
and thou, late so beauteous, wilt be a lifeless corpse.' The first
light of morning cheerfully illumined the dell; but Albert's
heart was not gladdened by the scene.

The beams of the sun began to gild the turrets of Werdendorff, yet the bridal ball was not concluded. In vain the blaze of
beauty met Lord Albert's eyes; he sighed amid surrounding
splendour; for conscience had strongly entwined her chains
around his heart. Guimilda was impatient to know if her lord
had accomplished the dire deed; and, on his answering in the
affirmative, she experienced the most extravagant and unnatural transports. But Albert was clouded with horror; and he

kept constantly repeating the words, 'At midnight's dark hour thou shalt embrace me again.'

On the next evening the guests again assembled in the halls of Werdendorff, again the musicians tuned their instruments to notes of joy; and again the gay knights and their fair partners joined in the mazy dance. Lord Albert alone seemed abstracted; and his woe-expressive countenance gave rise to a variety of conjectures, all very remote from the truth. Guimilda perceived the agony of his mind (which her hardened heart considered as a weakness) with extreme displeasure; nor was she slow in whispering to him the most keen reproaches for the pusillanimity of his conduct, in appearing in this manner before their guests.

But in vain Lord Albert endeavoured to arouse himself, and put on a gay unembarrassed air. His mind, in a few hours, had undergone a total revolution. He now regarded Guimilda as an agent of infernal malice, sent to plunge his soul into an irremediable abyss of guilt. The artless behaviour of his murdered love was the contrast; her gentle unupbraiding manners, the affectionate looks with which she would hang enraptured over him, and listen to the tender oaths he had so basely violated, was in these thoughts; yet they every moment rushed unbidden on his brain.

As midnight's dark hour was proclaimed by the turret bell, Albert's limbs shook with fear. 'I hear,' said he, aloud, 'the fatal summons that calls me hence. Guimilda, farewell for ever! this is thy work.'

Guimilda was going to make some reply, when a tremendous storm suddenly shook the battlements of the castle: the thunder's loud peals burst on the ancient walls, while the lightning's pointed glare flashed with appalling repetition through the painted casements. Dim burnt the numberless tapers, when Josephine's death-like form glided from the portal, and, with solemn pace, proceeded along the hall to the spot where Lord

Albert stood. Pale was her face, and her features seemed to retain the convulsive marks of the horrid death to which Guimilda had revengefully consigned her. Clad in the habiliments of the grave, her appearance was awe-inspiring. In a hollow, deep-toned voice, she addressed her perjured lover:

'Thou false one! Base assassin of her whom thou lured'st from the flowery paths of virtue; her whom thou had'st sworn to cherish and protect while life was left thee. Thou hast cut short the thread of my existence: but think not to escape the punishment due to thy crimes. 'Tis midnight's dark hour; the hour by thyself appointed: delay not, therefore, thy promised embrace.'

With these words Josephine wound her arms around his trembling form. 'I am come from the confines of the dead,' said she, 'to make thee fulfil thy parting promise.' She dragged him by a force he could not resist to her breast: she pressed her clammy lips to his; and held him fast in her noisome icy embrace.

At length the horrific spectre released him from her grasp. He started back in breathless agony, and sank senseless on the floor. Thrice he raised his frenzied eye to gaze on his supernatural visitant; thrice he raised his hands, as if to implore the mercy of offended heaven; and then expired with a heavy groan.

Again loud thunder shook the castle to its very foundation. The affrighted guests rushed from the hall, rather choosing to brave the fury of the elements, than remain spectators of the horrid scene within its walls. Even the proud Guimilda fled with terror and dismay. She sought refuge in a convent that stood about a league's distance from the castle; here she remained till death put a period to her mental sufferings, which far exceeded her corporeal ones; though they were many, and severe; for she exhausted her frame by the variety and frequencies of the vigorous penance she imposed on herself, as a chastisement for her heinous, regretted crime.

As soon as Lord Albert's body was interred, the domestics hastily left the horrid castle. The edifice, being greatly damaged by the storm, soon fell to decay. Its dismantled ramparts were skirted with thorns; and the proud turrets of Werdendorff lay scattered on the plain.

Full oft, when the traveller wanders among the time-stricken ruins, a peasant will lead him to his cot, and relate the sad story of Albert and Josephine, and warn the stranger not to rove among the avenues of the castle, lest he should be assailed by the grim spectres, who always punish the temerity of those who intrude with unhallowed steps in the mansion where they keep their mysterious orgies. The hall of the castle still remains entire amid the Gothic ruins. On the anniversary of that fatal night when Josephine's spectre gave the midnight embrace to the false Albert, the same scene is again acted by supernatural beings. Guimilda, her husband, and his murdered love, traverse the haunted hall, which is then illumined with a more than mortal light: and the groans of the spectre lord can be heard afar, while he is clasped in the arms of Josephine's implacable ghost.

Oft will the village maidens, at the sober gloom of evening, review the isolated scene, and relate to those of their juvenile companions, yet unacquainted with the tragic tale, all the particulars of that wondrous legend; while they shuddering pass the mouldering tomb that covers the libertine's remains, to weep over the lowly violet-covered grave of the fair, but frail Josephine.

The Demon of the Hartz

or

The Three Charcoal Burners

Thomas Peckett Prest

THE solitudes of the Hartz forest in Germany, but especially the mountains called Blockberg, or rather Blockenberg, are the chosen scene for tales of witches, demons, and apparitions. The occupation of the inhabitants, who are either miners or foresters, is of a kind that renders them peculiarly prone to superstition, and the natural phenomena which they witness in pursuit of their solitary or subterraneous profession, are often set down by them to the interference of goblins or the power of magic. Among the various legends current in that wild country, there is a favourite one which supposes the Hartz to be haunted by a sort of tutelar demon, in the shape of a wild man, of huge stature, his head wreathed with oak leaves, and his middle tinctured with the same, bearing in his hand a pine torn up by the root. It is certain that many persons profess to have seen such a man traversing, with huge strides, the opposite ridge of a mountain, when divided from it by a narrow glen; and indeed the fact of the apparition is so generally admitted, that modern scepticism has only found refuge by ascribing it to optical deception.

In elder times, the intercourse of the demon with the inhabitants was more familiar, and, according to the traditions of the Hartz, he was wont, with the caprice usually ascribed to these earth-born powers to interfere with the affairs of mortals, sometimes for their welfare. But it was observed, that even his gifts often turned out, in the long run, fatal to those on whom they were bestowed, and it was no uncommon thing for the pastors, in their care for their flock, to compose long sermons the

*See *The Midnight People*, ed. Peter Haining. Leslie Frewin, (U.K.), 1968; Grosset & Dunlap (U.S.-retitled Vampires at Midnight), 1970.

burthen whereof was a warning against having any intercourse, direct or indirect, with the Hartz demon. The fortunes of Martin Waldeck have been often quoted by the aged to their giddy children, when they were heard to scoff at a danger which appeared visionary.

A travelling capuchin had possessed himself of the pulpit of the thatched church at a little hamlet called Morgenbrodt, lying in the Hartz district, from which he declaimed against the wickedness of the inhabitants, their communication with fiends, witches, and fairies, and particularly with the woodland goblin of the Hartz. The doctrines of Luther had already begun to spread among the peasantry, for the incident is placed under the reign of Charles V, and they laughed to scorn the zeal with which the venerable man insisted upon his topic. At length, as his vehemence increased with opposition, so their opposition rose in proportion to his vehemence. The inhabitants did not like to hear an accustomed demon, who had inhabited the Brockenberg for so many ages, summarily confounded with Baal-peor, Ashtaroth, and Beelzebub himself, and condemned without reprieve to the bottomless Tophet. The apprehensions that the spirit might avenge himself on them for listening to such an illiberal sentence, added to the national interest in his behalf. A travelling friar, they said, that is here today and away tomorrow, may say what he pleases, but it is we the ancient and constant inhabitants of the country, that are left at the mercy of the insulted demon, and must, of course, pay for all. Under the irritation occasioned by these reflections the peasants from injurious language betook themselves to stones, and having pebbled the priest most handsomely, they drove him out of the parish to preach against demons elsewhere.

Three young men, who had been present and assisting in the attack upon the priest, carried on the laborious and mean occupation of preparing charcoal for the smelting furnaces. On their return to their hut, their conversation naturally turned upon the demon of the Hartz and the doctrine of the capuchin. Maximilian and George Waldeck, the two elder brothers, although they allowed the language of the capuchin to have been indiscreet and worthy of censure, as presuming to determine upon the precise character and abode of the spirit, yet contended it was dangerous, in the highest degree, to accept his gifts, or hold any communication with him. He was powerful they allowed, but wayward and capricious, and those who had intercourse with him seldom came to a good end. Did he not give the brave knight, Ecbert of Rabenwald, that famous black steed, by means of which he vanquished all the champions at the great tournament at Bremen? and did not the same steed afterwards precipitate itself with its rider into an abyss so deep and fearful, that neither horse nor man was ever seen more? Had he not given to Dame Gertrude Trodden a curious spell for making butter come? and was she not burnt for a witch by the grand criminal judge of the Electorate, because she availed herself of his gift? But these, and many other instances which they quoted, of mischance and ill-luck ultimately attending upon the apparent benefits conferred by the Hartz spirit, failed to make any impression on Martin Waldeck, the youngest of the brothers.

Martin was youthful, rash, and impetuous; excelling in all the exercises which distinguish a mountaineer, and brave and undaunted from the familiar intercourse with the dangers that attend them. He laughed at the timidity of his brothers. 'Tell me not of such folly,' he said; 'the demon is a good demon – he lives among us as if he were a peasant like ourselves – haunts the lonely crags or recesses of the mountains like a huntsman or goatherd – and he who loves the Hartz-forest and its wild scenes cannot be indifferent to the fate of the hardy children of the soil. But if the demon were as malicious as you make him, how should he derive power over mortals who barely avail themselves of his gifts, without binding themselves to submit to his pleasure? When you carry your charcoal to the furnace, is not the money as good that is paid you by blaspheming Blaize, the old reprobate overseer, as if you got it from the pastor himself? It is not the goblin's gifts which can endanger you then, but it is the use you shall make of them that you must account for.

And were the demon to appear at this moment, and indicate to me a gold or silver mine, I would begin to dig away before his back were turned, and I would consider myself as under protection of a much Greater than he, while I made a good use of the wealth he pointed out to me.'

To this the elder brother replied, that wealth ill won was seldom well spent, while Martin presumptuously declared, that the possession of all the Hartz would not make the slightest alteration on his habits, morals, or character.

His brother entreated Martin to talk less wildly upon this subject, and with some difficulty contrived to withdraw his attention, by calling it to the consideration of an approaching boar-chase. This talk brought them to their hut, a wretched wigwam, situated upon one side of a wild, narrow, and romantic dell in the recesses of the Brockenberg. They released their sister from attending upon the operation of charring the wood, which requires constant attention, and divided among themselves the duty of watching it by night, according to their custom, one always waking while his brothers slept.

Max Waldeck, the eldest, watched during the two first hours of night, and was considerably alarmed, by observing upon the opposite bank of the glen, or valley a huge fire surrounded by some figures that appeared to wheel around it with antic gestures. Max at first bethought him of calling up his brothers; but recollecting the daring character of the youngest, and finding it impossible to wake the elder without also disturbing him – conceiving also what he saw to be an illusion of the demon, sent perhaps in consequence of the venturous expressions used by Martin on the preceding evening, he thought it best to betake himself to the safe-guard of such prayers as he could murmur over, and to watch in great terror and annoyance this strange and alarming apparition. After blazing for some time, the fire faded gradually away into darkness, and the rest of Max's watch was only disturbed by the remembrance of its terrors.

George now occupied the place of Max, who had retired to rest. The phenomenon of a huge blazing fire, upon the opposite bank of the glen, again presented itself to the eye of the watchman. It was surrounded as before by figures, which, distinguished by their opaque forms, being between the spectator and the red glaring light, moved and fluctuated around it as if engaged in some mystical ceremonies. George, though equally cautious, was of a bolder character than his elder brother. He resolved to examine more nearly the object of his wonder; and accordingly, after crossing the rivulet which divided the glen, he climbed up the opposite bank, and approached within an arrow's flight from the fire, which blazed apparently with the same fury as when he first witnessed it.

The appearance of the assistants who surrounded it, resembled those phantoms which are seen in a troubled dream, and at once confirmed the idea he had entertained from the first, that they did not belong to the human world. Amongst the strange unearthly forms, George Waldeck distinguished that of a giant overgrown with hair, holding an uprooted fir in his hand, with which, from time to time, he seemed to stir the blazing fire and having no other clothing than a wreath of oak leaves round his forehead and loins. George's heart sunk within him at recognizing the well-known apparition of the Hartz demon, as he had often been described to him by the ancient shepherds and huntsmen who had seen his form traversing the mountains. He turned, and was about to fly; but, upon second thoughts, blaming his own cowardice, he recited mentally the verse of the Psalmist, 'All good angels praise the Lord!' which is in that country supposed powerful as an exorcism and turned himself once more towards the place where he had seen the fire. But it was no longer visible.

The pale moon alone enlightened the side of the valley, and when George, with trembling steps, a moist brow, and hair bristling upright under his collier's cap, came to the spot where the fire had been so lately visible, marked as it was by a scathed oak tree, there appeared not on the heath the slightest vestiges of what he had seen. The moss and wild flowers were unscorched, and the branches of the oak tree, which had so lately appeared enveloped in wreaths of flame and smoke, were moist with the dews of midnight.

George returned to his hut with trembling steps, and, arguing like his elder brother, resolved to say nothing of what he had seen, lest he should awake in Martin that daring curiosity which he almost deemed to be allied with impiety.

It was now Martin's turn to watch. The household cock had given his first summons, and the night was well nigh spent. On examining the state of the furnace in which the wood was deposited in order to its being coked, or charred, he was surprised to find that the fire had not been sufficiently maintained; for in his excursion and its consequences, George had forgot the principal object of his watch. Martin's first thought was to call up the slumberers, but observing that both his brothers slept unwontedly deep and heavily, he respected their repose, and set himself to supply their furnace with fuel, without requiring their aid. What he heaped upon it was apparently damp and unfit for the purpose, for the fire seemed rather to decay than revive. Martin next went to collect some boughs from a stack which had been carefully cut and dried for this purpose; but, when he returned, he found the fire totally extinguished. This was a serious evil, which threatened them with loss of their trade for more than one day. The vexed and mortified watchman set about to strike a light in order to rekindle the fire, but the tinder was moist, and his labour proved in this respect also ineffectual. He was now about to call up his brothers, for the circumstance seemed to be pressing, when flashes of light glimmered not only through the window, but through every crevice of the rudely built hut, and summoned him to behold the same apparition which had before alarmed the successive watches of his brethren. His first idea was, that the Muhllerhaussers, their rivals in trade, and with whom they had had many quarrels, might have encroached upon their bounds for the purpose of pirating their wood, and he resolved to awake his brothers, and be revenged on them for their audacity. But a short reflection and observation on the gestures and manner of those who seemed 'to work in the fire', induced him to dismiss this belief, and although rather sceptical in these matters, to conclude that what he saw was a supernatural phenomenon. 'But be they

men or fiends,' said the undaunted forester, 'that busy themselves yonder with such fantastical rites and gestures, I will go
and demand a light to rekindle our furnace.' He relinquished,
at the same time, the idea of waking his brethren. There was a
belief that such adventures as he was about to undertake were
accessible only to one person at a time; he feared also that
his brothers in their scrupulous timidity, might interfere to
prevent his pursuing the investigation he had resolved to com-
mence; and therefore, snatching his boar-spear from the wall,
the undaunted Martin Waldeck set forth on the adventure
alone.

With the same success as his brother George, but with courage far superior, Martin crossed the brook, ascended the hill,
and approached so near the ghostly assembly, that he could
recognize, in the presiding figure, the attributes of the Hartz
demon. A cold shuddering assailed him for the first time in his
life, but the recollection that he had at a distance dared and even
courted the intercourse which was now about to take place,
confirmed his staggering courage, and pride supplying what he
wanted in resolution, he advanced with tolerable firmness towards the fire, the figures which surrounded it appeared still
more phantastical, and supernatural, the nearer he approached
to the assembly. He was received with a loud shout of discordant and unnatural laughter, which, to his stunned ears, seemed
more alarming than a combination of the most dismal and
melancholy sounds which could be imagined. – 'Who art thou?'
said the giant compressing his savage and exaggerated features
into a sort of forced gravity, while they were occasionally agitated by the convulsion of the laughter which he seemed to sup-
press.

'Martin Waldeck the forester,' answered the hardy youth; –
'And who are you?'

'The king of the waste and of the mine,' answered the
spectre; –'And why hast thou dared to encroach on my mysteries?'

'I came in search of light to rekindle my fire,' answer Martin hardily, and then resolutely asked in his turn, 'What mys-

teries are these that you celebrate here?'

'We celebrate,' answered the demoniac being, 'the wedding of Hèrmes with the Black Dragon. – But take thy fire that thou camest to seek, and begone – No mortal may long look upon us and live.'

The peasant stuck his spear point into a large piece of blazing wood, which he heaved with some difficulty, and then turned round to regain his hut, the shouts of laughter being renewed behind him with treble violence, and ringing far down the narrow valley. When Martin returned to the hut, his first care, however much astonished with what he had seen, was to dispose the kindled coal among the fuel so as might best light the fire of his furnace, but after many efforts, and all exertions of bellows and fire-prong, the coal he had brought from the demon's fire became totally extinct, without kindling any of the others. He turned about and observed the fire still blazing on the hill, although those who had been busied around it had disappeared. As he conceived the spectre had been jesting with him, he gave way to the natural hardihood of his temper, and determining to see the adventure to the end, resumed the road to the fire, from which, unopposed by the demon, he brought off in the same manner a blazing piece of charcoal but still without being able to succeed in lighting his fire. Impunity having increased his rashness, he resolved upon a third experiment, and was as successful as before in reaching the fire; but, when he had again appropriated a piece of burning coal, and had turned to depart, he heard the harsh and supernatural voice which had before accosted him, pronounce these words, 'Dare not to return hither a fourth time!'

The attempt to rekindle the fire with this last coal having proved as ineffectual as on the former occasions, Martin relinquished the hopeless attempt, and flung himself on his bed of leaves, resolving to delay till the next morning the communication of his supernatural adventure to his brothers. He was awakened from a heavy sleep into which he had sunk, from fatigue of body and agitation of mind, by loud exclamations of joy and surprise. His brothers, astonished at finding the fire extinguished when they awoke, had proceeded to arrange the fuel in order to renew it, when they found in the ashes three huge metallic masses, which their skill, (for most of the peasants in the Hartz are practised mineralogists,) immediately ascertained to be pure gold.

It was some damp upon their joyful congratulations when they learned from Martin the mode in which he had obtained his treasure, to which their own experience of the nocturnal vision induced them to give full credit. But they were unable to resist the temptation of sharing their brother's wealth. Taking now upon him as head of the house, Martin Waldeck bought lands and forests, built a castle, obtained a patent of nobility, and greatly to the scorn of the ancient nobility of the neighbourhood, was invested with all the privileges of a man of family. His courage in public war, as well as in private feuds, together with the number of retainers whom he kept in pay, sustained him for some time against the odium which was excited by his sudden elevation, and the arrogance of his pretensions. And now it was seen in the instance of Martin Waldeck, as it has been in that of many others, how little mortals can foresee the effect of sudden prosperity on their own disposition. The evil dispositions in his nature, which poverty had checked and repressed, ripened and bore their un-allowed fruit under the influence of temptation and the means of indulgence. As Deep calls unto Deep, one bad passion awakened another : – the fiend of avarice invoked that of pride, and pride was to be supported by cruelty and oppression. Waldeck's character, always bold and daring, but rendered more harsh and assuming by prosperity, soon made him odious, not to nobles only, but likewise to the lower ranks, who saw, with double dislike, the oppressive rights of the feudal nobility of the empire so remorselessly exercised by one who had risen from the very dregs of the people. His adventure, although carefully concealed, began likewise to be whispered, and the clergy already stigmatized as a wizard and accomplice of fiends, the wretch, who, having acquired so huge a treasure in so strange a manner had not sought to sanctify it by dedicating a considerable portion to the use of the church. Surrounded by enemies, public and private, tormented by a thousand feuds, and threatened by the church with excommunication, Martin Waldeck, or, as we must now call him the Baron Von Waldeck, often regretted bitterly the labours and sports of unenvied poverty. But his courage failed him not under all these difficulties and seemed rather to augment in proportion to the danger which darkened around him until an accident precipitated his fall.

A proclamation by the reigning Duke of Brunswick had invited to a solemn tournament all German nobles of free and honourable descent, and Martin Waldeck, splendidly armed accompanied by his two brothers, and a gallantly equipped retinue, had the arrogance to appear among the chivalry of the province and demand permission to enter the lists. This was considered as filling up the measure of his presumption. A thousand voices exclaimed, 'we will have no cinder-sifter mingle in our games of chivalry.' Irritated to frenzy, Martin drew his sword, and hewed down the herald who, in compliance with the general outcry, opposed his entrance into the list. A hundred swords were unsheathed to avenge what was, in those days, regarded as a crime only inferior to sacrilege, or regicide. Waldeck, after defending himself with the fury of a lion, was seized, tried on the spot by the judges of the lists, and condemned, as the appropriate punishment for breaking the peace of his sovereign and violating the sacred person of a herald-at-arms, to have his right hand struck from his body, to be ignominiously deprived of the honour of nobility, of which he was unworthy, and be expelled from the city. When he had been stripped of his arms, and sustained the mutilation imposed by this severe sentence, the unhappy victim of ambition was abandoned to the rabble, who followed him with threats and outcries, levelled alternately against the necromancer and oppressor, which at length ended in violence. His brothers, (for his retinue had fled and dispersed) at length succeeded in rescuing him from the hands of the populace, when, satiated with cruelty, they had left him half dead through loss of blood, through the outrages he had sustained. They were not permitted, such was the ingenious cruelty of their enemies, to make use of any other means of removing him, excepting such a collier's cart as they had themselves formerly used, in which they deposited their brother on a truss of straw, scarcely expecting to reach any place of shelter ere death should release him from his misery.

When the Waldecks, journeying in this miserable manner, had approached the verge of their native country, in a hollow way, between two mountains, they perceived a figure advancing towards them, which at first sight seemed to be an aged man. But as he approached, his limbs and stature increased, the cloak fell from his shoulders, his pilgrim's staff was changed into an uprooted pine tree, and the gigantic figure of the Hartz demon passed before them in his terrors. When he came opposite to the cart which contained the miserable Waldeck, his huge features dilated into a grin of unutterable contempt and malignity, as he asked the sufferer, 'How like you the fire MY coals have kindled?' The power of motion, which terror suspended in his two brothers, seemed to be restored to Martin by the energy of his courage. He raised himself on the cart, bent his brows, and, clenching his fist, shook it at the spectre with a ghastly look of hate and defiance. The goblin vanished with his usual tremendous and explosive laugh and left Waldeck exhausted with the effort of expiring nature.

The terrified brethren turned their vehicle towards the towers of a convent which arose in a wood of pine trees beside the road. They were charitably received by a bare-footed and long-bearded capuchin, and Martin survived only to complete the first confession he had made since the day of his sudden prosperity, and to receive absolution from the very priest, whom, precisely that day three years, he had assisted to pelt out of the hamlet of Morgenbrodt. The three years of precarious prosperity were supposed to have a mysterious correspondence with the number of his visits to the spectral fire upon the hill.

The body of Martin Waldeck was interred in the convent where he expired, in which his brothers, having assumed the habit of the order, lived and died in the performance of acts of charity and devotion. His lands, to which no one asserted any claim, lay waste until they were reassumed by the emperor as a lapsed fief, and the ruins of the castle, which Waldeck had called by his own name, are still shunned by the miner and forester as haunted by evil spirits. Thus were the evils attendant upon wealth, hastily attained and ill-employed, exemplified in the fortunes of Martin Waldeck.

Gabriel-Ernest

Saki

'There is a wild beast in your woods,' said the artist Cunning-ham, as he was being driven to the station. It was the only remark he had made during the drive, but as Van Cheele had talked incessantly his companion's silence had not been notice-able.

'A stray fox or two and some resident weasels. Nothing more formidable,' said Van Cheele. The artist said nothing.

'What did you mean about a wild beast?' said Van Cheele later, when they were on the platform.

'Nothing. My imagination. Here is the train,' said Cunning-ham.

That afternoon Van Cheele went for one of his frequent rambles through his woodland property. He had a stuffed bittern in his study, and knew the names of quite a number of wild flowers, so his aunt had possibly some justification in describing him as a great naturalist. At any rate, he was a great walker. It was his custom to take mental notes of everything he saw during his walks, not so much for the purpose of assisting contemporary science as to provide topics for conversation afterwards. When the bluebells began to show themselves in flower he made a point of informing everyone of the fact; the season of the year might have warned his hearers of the likeli-hood of such an occurrence, but at least they felt that he was being absolutely frank with them.

What Van Cheele saw on this particular afternoon was, however, something far removed from his ordinary range of experience. On a shelf of smooth stone overhanging a deep pool in the hollow of an oak coppice a boy of about sixteen lay asprawl, drying his wet brown limbs luxuriously in the sun. His wet hair, parted by a recent dive, lay close to his head, and his light-brown eyes, so light that there was an almost tigerish gleam in them, were turned towards Van Cheele with a certain lazy watchfulness. It was an unexpected apparition, and Van Cheele found himself engaged in the novel process of thinking before he spoke. Where on earth could this wild-looking boy hail from? The miller's wife had lost a child some two months ago, supposed to have been swept away by the mill-race,but that had been a mere baby, not a half-grown lad.

'What are you doing there?' he demanded.

'Obviously, sunning myself,' replied the boy.

'Where do you live?'

'Here, in these woods.'

'You can't live in the woods,' said Van Cheele.

'They are very nice woods,' said the boy, with a touch of patronage in his voice.

'But where do you sleep at night?'

'I don't sleep at night; that's my busiest time.'

Van Cheele began to have an irritated feeling that he was grappling with a problem that was eluding him.

'What do you feed on?' he asked.

'Flesh,' said the boy, and he pronounced the word with slow relish, as though he were tasting it.

'Flesh! What flesh?'

'Since it interests you, rabbits, wild-fowl, hares, poultry, lambs in their season, children when I can get any; they're usually too well locked in at night, when I do most of my hunting. It's quite two months since I tasted child-flesh.'

Ignoring the chaffing nature of the last remark, Van Cheele tried to draw the boy on the subject of possible poaching operations.

'You're talking rather through your hat when you speak of feeding on hares.' (Considering the nature of the boy's toilet, the smile was hardly an apt one.) 'Our hillside hares aren't easily caught.'

'At night I hunt on four feet,' was the somewhat cryptic response.

'I suppose you mean that you hunt with a dog?' hazarded Van Cheele.

The boy rolled slowly over on to his back, and laughed a weird low laugh, that was pleasantly like a chuckle and disagreeably like a snarl.

'I don't fancy any dog would be very anxious for my company, especially at night.'

Van Cheele began to feel that there was something positively uncanny about the strange-eyed, strange-tongued youngster.

'I can't have you staying in these woods,' he declared authoritatively.

'I fancy you'd rather have me here than in your house,' said the boy.

The prospect of this wild, nude animal in Van Cheele's primly ordered house was certainly an alarming one.

'If you don't go I shall have to make you,' said Van Cheele.

The boy turned like a flash, plunged into the pool, and in a moment had flung his wet and glistening body half-way up the bank where Van Cheele was standing. In an otter the movement would not have been remarkable; in a boy Van Cheele found it sufficiently startling. His foot slipped as he made an involuntary backward movement, and he found himself almost prostrate on the slippery weed-grown bank, with those tigerish yellow eyes not very far from his own. Almost instinctively he half-raised his hand to his throat. The boy laughed again, a laugh in which the snarl had nearly driven out the chuckle, and then, with another of his astonishing lightning movements, plunged out of view into a yielding tangle of weed and fern.

'What an extraordinary wild animal!' said Van Cheele as he picked himself up. And then he recalled Cunningham's remark, 'There is a wild beast in your woods.'

Walking slowly homeward, Van Cheele began to turn over in his mind various local occurrences which might be traceable to the existence of this astonishing young savage.

Something had been thinning the game in the woods lately, poultry had been missing from the farms, hares were growing unaccountably scarcer, and complaints had reached him of lambs being carried off bodily from the hills. Was it possible that this wild boy was really hunting the countryside in company with some clever poacher dog? He had spoken of hunting 'four-footed' by night, but then, again, he had hinted strangely at no dog caring to come near him, 'especially at night'. It was certainly puzzling. And then, as Van Cheele ran his mind over the various depredations that had been committed during the last month or two, he came suddenly to a dead stop, alike in his walk and his speculations. The child missing from the mill two months ago – the accepted theory was that it had tumbled into the mill race and been swept away; but the mother had always declared she had heard a shriek on the hill side of the house, in the opposite direction from the water. It was unthinkable, of course, but he wished that the boy had not made that uncanny remark about child-flesh eaten two months ago. Such dreadful things should not be said even in fun.

Van Cheele, contrary to his usual wont, did not feel disposed to be communicative about his discovery in the wood. His position as a parish councillor and justice of the peace seemed somehow compromised by the fact that he was harbouring a personality of such doubtful repute on his property; there was even a possibility that a heavy bill of damages for raided lambs and poultry might be laid at his door. At dinner that night he was quite unusually silent.

'Where's your voice gone to?' said his aunt. 'One would think you had seen a wolf.'

Van Cheele, who was not familiar with the old saying, thought the remark rather foolish; if he *had* seen a wolf on his property his tongue would have been extraordinarily busy with the subject.

At breakfast next morning Van Cheele was conscious that his feeling of uneasiness regarding yesterday's episode had not wholly disappeared, and he resolved to go by train to the neighbouring cathedral town, hunt up Cunningham, and learn from him what he had really seen that had prompted the remark about a wild beast in the woods. With this resolution taken, his usual cheerfulness partially returned, and he hummed a bright little melody as he sauntered to the morning-room for his customary cigarette. As he entered the room the melody made way abruptly for a pious invocation. Gracefully asprawl on the ottoman, in an attitude of almost exaggerated repose, was the boy of the woods. He was drier than when Van Cheele had last seen him, but no other alteration was noticeable in his toilet.

'How dare you come here?' asked Van Cheele furiously.

'You told me I was not to stay in the woods,' said the boy calmly.

'But not to come here. Supposing my aunt should see you!'

And with a view to minimising that catastrophe Van Cheele hastily obscured as much of his unwelcome guest as possible under the folds of a *Morning Post*. At that moment his aunt entered the room.

'This is a poor boy who has lost his way – and lost his memory. He doesn't know who he is or where he comes from,' explained Van Cheele desperately, glancing apprehensively at the waif's face to see whether he was going to add inconvenient candour to his other savage propensities.

Miss Van Cheele was enormously interested.

'Perhaps his underlinen is marked,' she suggested.

'He seems to have lost most of that, too,' said Van Cheele, making frantic little grabs at the *Morning Post* to keep it in its place.

A naked homeless child appealed to Miss Van Cheele as warmly as a stray kitten or derelict puppy would have done.

'We must do all we can for him,' she decided, and in a very short time a messenger, dispatched to the rectory, where a page-boy was kept, had returned with a suit of pantry clothes, and the necessary accessories of shirt, shoes, collar, etc. Clothed, clean, and groomed, the boy lost none of his uncanniness in Van Cheele's eyes, but his aunt found him sweet.

'We must call him something till we know who he really is,' she said. 'Gabriel-Ernest, I think; those are nice suitable names.'

Van Cheele agreed, but he privately doubted whether they were being grafted on to a nice suitable child. His misgivings were not diminished by the fact that his staid and elderly spaniel had bolted out of the house at the first incoming of the boy, and now obstinately remained shivering and yapping at the farther end of the orchard, while the canary, usually as vocally industrious as Van Cheele himself, had put itself on an allowance of frightened cheeps. More than ever he was resolved to consult Cunningham without loss of time.

As he drove off to the station his aunt was arranging that Gabriel-Ernest should help her to entertain the infant members of her Sunday-school class at tea that afternoon.

Cunningham was not at first disposed to be communicative.

'My mother died of some brain trouble,' he explained, 'so you will understand why I am averse to dwelling on anything of an impossibly fantastic nature that I may see or think that I have seen.'

'But what *did* you see?' persisted Van Cheele.

'What I thought I saw was something so extraordinary that no really sane man could dignify it with the credit of having actually happened. I was standing, the last evening I was with you, half-hidden in the hedgegrowth by the orchard gate, watching the dying glow of the sunset. Suddenly I became aware of a naked boy, a bather from some neighbouring pool, I took him to be, who was standing out on the bare hillside also watching the sunset. His pose was so suggestive of some wild faun of Pagan myth that I instantly wanted to engage him as a model, and in another moment I think I should have hailed him. But just then the sun dipped out of view, and all the orange and pink slid of the landscape, leaving it cold and grey. And at the same moment an astounding thing happened – the boy vanished too!'

'What! vanished away into nothing?' asked Van Cheele excitedly.

'No; that is the dreadful part of it,' answered the artist; 'on the open hillside where the boy had been standing a second ago, stood a large wolf, blackish in colour, with gleaming fangs and cruel, yellow eyes. You may think—'

But Van Cheele did not stop for anything as futile as thought.

Already he was tearing at top speed towards the station. He dismissed the idea of a telegram. 'Gabriel-Ernest is a werewolf' was a hopelessly inadequate effort at conveying the situation, and his aunt would think it was a code message to which he had omitted to give her the key. His one hope was that he might reach home before sundown. The cab which he chartered at the other end of the railway journey bore him with what seemed exasperating slowness along the country roads, which were pink and mauve with the flush of the sinking sun. His aunt was putting away some unfinished jams and cake when he arrived.

'Where is Gabriel-Ernest?' he almost screamed.

'He is taking the little Toop child home,' said his aunt. 'It was getting so late, I thought it wasn't safe to let it go back alone. What a lovely sunset, isn't it?'

But Van Cheele, although not oblivious of the glow in the western sky, did not stay to discuss its beauties. At a speed for which he was scarcely geared he raced along the narrow lane that led to the home of the Toops. On one side ran the swift current of the mill-stream, on the other rise the stretch of bare hillside. A dwindling rim of red sun showed still on the skyline, and the next turning must bring him in view of the ill-assorted couple he was pursuing. Then the colour went suddenly out of things, and a grey light settled itself with a quick shiver over the landscape. Van Cheele heard a shrill wail of fear, and stopped running.

Nothing was ever seen again of the Toop child or Gabriel-Ernest, but the latter's discarded garments were found lying in the road, so it was assumed that the child had fallen into the water, and that the boy had stripped and jumped in, in a vain endeavour to save it. Van Cheele and some workmen who were near by at the time testified to having heard a child scream loudly just near the spot where the clothes were found. Mrs Toop, who had eleven other children, was decently resigned to her bereavement, but Miss Van Cheele sincerely mourned her lost foundling. It was on her initiative that a memorial brass was put up in the parish church to 'Gabriel-Ernest, an unknown boy, who bravely sacrificed his life for another.'

Van Cheele gave way to his aunt in most things, but he flatly refused to subscribe to the Gabriel-Ernest memorial.

The White Wolf of the Hartz Mountains

CAPTAIN FREDERICK MARRYAT

Before noon Philip and Krantz had embarked, and made sail in the peroqua.

They had no difficulty in steering their course; the islands by day, and the clear stars by night, were their compass. It is true that they did not follow the more direct track, but they followed the more secure, working up through the smooth waters, and gaining to the northward more than to the west. Many times were they chased by the Malay proas, which infested the islands, but the swiftness of their little peroqua was their security; indeed the chase was, generally speaking, abandoned, as soon as the smallness of the vessel was made out by the pirates, who expected that little or no booty was to be gained.

One morning, as they were sailing between the isles, with less wind than usual, Philip observed: 'Krantz, you said that there were events in your own life, or connected with it, which would corroborate the mysterious tale I confided to you. Will you now tell me to what you referred?'

'Certainly,' replied Krantz; 'I have often thought of doing so, but one circumstance or another has hitherto prevented me; this is, however, a fitting opportunity. Prepare therefore to listen to a strange story, quite as strange, perhaps, as your own.

'I take it for granted, that you have heard people speak of the Hartz Mountains,' observed Krantz.

'I have never heard people speak of them that I can recollect,' replied Philip; 'but I have read of them in some book, and of the strange things which have occurred there.'

'It is indeed a wild region,' rejoined Krantz, 'and many strange tales are told of it; but, strange as they are, I have good reason for believing them to be true. I have told you, Philip, that I fully believe in your communion with the other world – that I credit the history of your father, and the lawfulness of your mission; for that we are surrounded, impelled, and worked upon by beings different in their nature from ourselves, I have had full evidence, as you will acknowledge, when I state what has occurred in my own family. Why such malevolent beings as I am about to speak of should be permitted to interfere with us, and punish, I may say, comparatively unoffending mortals, is beyond my comprehension; but that they are so permitted is most certain.'

'The great principle of all evil fulfils his work of evil; why, then, not the other minor spirits of the same class?' inquired Philip. 'What matters it to us, whether we are tried by, and have to suffer from, the enmity of our fellow-mortals, or whether we are persecuted by beings more powerful and more malevolent than ourselves? We know that we have to work out our salvation, and that we shall be judged according to our strength; if then there be evil spirits who delight to oppress man, there surely must be, as Amine asserts, good spirits, whose delight is to do him service. Whether, then, we have to struggle against our passions only, or whether we have to struggle not only against our passions, but also the dire influence of unseen enemies, we ever struggle with the same odds in our favour, as the good are stronger than the evil which we combat. In either case we are on the 'vantage ground, whether, as in the first, we fight the good cause single-handed, or as in the second, although opposed, we have the host of Heaven ranged on our side. Thus are the scales of Divine Justice evenly balanced, and man is still a free agent, as his own virtuous or vicious propensities must ever decide whether he shall gain or lose the victory.'

'Most true,' replied Krantz, 'and now to my history.

'My father was not born, or originally a resident, in the Hartz Mountains; he was the serf of an Hungarian nobleman, of great possessions, in Transylvania; but, although a serf, he was not by any means a poor or illiterate man. In fact, he was rich, and his intelligence and respectability were such, that he had been raised by his lord to the stewardship; but, whoever may happen to be born a serf, a serf must he remain, even though he become a wealthy man; such was the condition of my father. My father had been married for about five years; and, by his marriage, had three children – my eldest brother Caesar, myself (Hermann), and a sister named Marcella. You know, Philip, that Latin is still the language spoken in that country; and that will account for our high-sounding names. My mother was a very beautiful woman, unfortunately more beautiful than virtuous: she was seen and admired by the lord of the soil; my father was sent away upon some mission; and, during his absence, my mother, flattered by the attentions, and won by the assiduities, of this nobleman, yielded to his wishes. It so happened that my father returned very unexpectedly, and discovered the intrigue. The evidence of my mother's shame was positive: he surprised her in the company of her seducer! Carried away by the impetuosity of his feelings, he watched the opportunity of a meeting taking place between them, and murdered both his wife and her seducer. Conscious that, as a serf, not even the provocation which he had received would be allowed as a justification of his conduct, he hastily collected together what money he could lay his hands upon, and, as we were then in the depth of winter, he put his horses to the sleigh, and taking his children with him, he set off in the middle of the night, and was far away before the tragical circumstance had transpired. Aware that he would be pursued, and that he had no chance of escape if he remained in any portion of his native country (in which the authorities could lay hold of him), he continued his flight without intermission until he had buried himself in the intricacies and seclusion of the Hartz Mountains. Of course, all that I have now told you I learned afterwards. My oldest recollections are knit to a rude, yet comfortable cottage, in which I lived with my father, brother, and sister. It was on the confines of one of those vast forests which cover the northern part of Germany; around it were a few acres of ground, which, during the summer months, my father cultivated, and which, though they yielded a doubtful harvest, were sufficient for our support. In the winter we remained much indoors, for, as my father followed the chase, we were left alone, and the wolves, during that season, incessantly prowled about. My father had purchased the cottage, and land about it, of one of the rude foresters, who gain their livelihood partly by hunting, and partly by burning charcoal, for the purpose of smelting the ore from the neighbouring mines; it was distant about two miles from any other habitation. I can call to mind the whole landscape now: the tall pines which rose up on the mountain above us, and the wide expanse of forest beneath, on the topmost boughs and heads of whose trees we looked down from our cottage, as the mountain below us rapidly descended into the distant valley. In summertime the prospect was beautiful; but during the severe winter, a more desolate scene could not well be imagined.

'I said that, in the winter, my father occupied himself with the chase; every day he left us, and often would he lock the door, that we might not leave the cottage. He had no-one to assist him, or to take care of us – indeed, it was not easy to find a female servant who would live in such a solitude; but, could he have found one, my father would not have received her, for he had imbibed a horror of the sex, as the difference of his conduct towards us, his two boys, and my poor little sister, Marcella, evidently proved. You may suppose we were sadly neglected; indeed, we suffered much, for my father, fearful that we might come to some harm, would not allow us fuel, when he left the cottage; and we were obliged, therefore, to creep under the heaps of bears'-skins, and there to keep ourselves as warm as we could until he returned in the evening, when a blazing fire was our delight. That my father chose this restless sort of life may appear strange, but the fact was that he could not remain quiet; whether from remorse for having committed murder, or from the misery consequent on his change of situation, or from both combined, he was never happy unless he was in a state of activity. Children, however, when left much to themselves, acquire a thoughtfulness not common to their age. So it was with us; and during the short cold days of winter we would sit silent, longing for the happy hours when the snow would melt, and the leaves burst out, and the birds begin their songs, and when we should again be set at liberty.

'Such was our peculiar and savage sort of life until my brother Caesar was nine, myself seven, and my sister five, years old, when the circumstances occurred on which is based the extraordinary narrative which I am about to relate.

'One evening my father returned home rather later than usual; he had been unsuccessful, and, as the weather was very severe, and many feet of snow were upon the ground, he was not only very cold, but in a very bad humour. He had brought in wood, and we were all three of us gladly assisting each other in blowing on the embers to create the blaze, when he caught poor little Marcella by the arm and threw her aside; the child fell, struck her mouth, and bled very much. My brother ran to raise her up. Accustomed to ill-usage, and afraid of my father, she did not dare to cry, but looked up in his face very piteously. My father drew his stool nearer to the hearth, muttered something in abuse of women, and busied himself with the fire, which both my brother and I had deserted when our sister was so unkindly treated. A cheerful blaze was soon the result of his exertions; but we did not, as usual, crowd round it. Marcella, still bleeding, retired to a corner, and my brother and I took our seats beside her, while my father hung over the fire gloomily and alone. Such had been our position for about half-an-hour, when the howl of a wolf, close under the window of the cottage, fell on our ears. My father started up, and seized his gun: the howl was repeated, he examined the priming, and then hastily left the cottage, shutting the door after him. We all waited (anxiously listening), for we thought that if he succeeded in shooting the wolf, he would return in a better humour; and although he was harsh to all of us, and particularly so to our little sister, still we loved our father, and loved to see him cheerful and happy, for what else had we to look up to? And I may here observe, that perhaps there never were three children who were fonder of each other; we did not, like other children, fight and dispute together; and if, by chance, any disagreement did arise between my elder brother and me, little Marcella would run to us, and kissing us both, seal, through her entreaties, the peace between us. Marcella was a lovely, amiable child; I can recall her beautiful features even now – Alas! poor little Marcella.'

'She is dead then?' observed Philip.

'Dead! Yes, dead! – but how did she die? – But I must not anticipate, Philip; let me tell my story.

'We waited for some time, but the report of the gun did not reach us, and my elder brother then said, 'Our father has followed the wolf, and will not be back for some time. Marcella, let us wash the blood from your mouth, and then we will leave this corner, and go to the fire and warm ourselves.'

'We did so, and remained there until near midnight, every minute wondering, as it grew later, why our father did not return. We had no idea that he was in any danger, but we thought that he must have chased the wolf for a very long time. 'I will look out and see if father is coming,' said my brother Caesar, going to the door.

'Take care,' said Marcella, 'the wolves must be about now, and we cannot kill them, brother.'

My brother opened the door very cautiously, and but a few inches; he peeped out. – 'I see nothing,' said he, after a time, and once more he joined us at the fire.

'We have had no supper,' said I, for my father usually cooked the meat as soon as he came home; and during his absence we had nothing but the fragments of the preceding day.

'And if our father comes home after his hunt, Caesar,' said Marcella, 'he will be pleased to have some supper; let us cook it for him and for ourselves.'

Caesar climbed upon the stool, and reached down some meat – I forget now whether it was venison or bear's meat; but we cut off the usual quantity, and proceeded to dress it, as we used to do under our father's superintendence. We were all busied putting it into the platters before the fire, to await his coming, when we heard the sound of a horn. We listened – there was a noise outside, and a minute afterwards my father entered, ushering in a young female, and a large dark man in a hunter's dress.

'Perhaps I had better now relate, what was only known to me many years afterwards. When my father had left the cottage, he perceived a large white wolf about thirty yards from him; as soon as the animal saw my father, it retreated slowly, growling and snarling. My father followed; the animal did not run, but always kept at some distance; and my father did not like to fire until he was pretty certain that his ball would take effect: thus they went on for some time, the wolf now leaving my father far behind, and then stopping and snarling defiance at him, and then again, on his approach, setting off at speed.

'Anxious to shoot the animal (for the white wolf is very rare), my father continued the pursuit for several hours, during which he continually ascended the mountain.

'You must know, Philip, that there are peculiar spots on those mountains which are supposed, and, as my story will prove, truly supposed, to be inhabited by the evil influences; they are well known to the huntsmen, who invariably avoid them. Now, one of these spots, an open space in the pine forests above us, had been pointed out to my father as dangerous on that account. But, whether he disbelieved these wild stories, or whether, in his eager pursuit of the chase, he disregarded them, I know not; certain, however, it is, that he was decoyed by the white wolf to this open space, when the animal appeared to slacken her speed. My father approached, came close up to her, raised his gun to his shoulder, and was about to fire; when the wolf suddenly disappeared. He thought that the snow on the ground must have dazzled his sight, and he let down his gun to look for the beast – but she was gone; how she could have escaped over the clearance, without his seeing her, was beyond his comprehension. Mortified at the ill success of his chase, he was about to retrace his steps, when he heard the distant sound of a horn. Astonishment at such a sound – at such an hour – in such a wilderness, made him forget for the moment his disappointment, and he remained riveted to the spot. In a minute the horn was blown a second time, and at no great distance; my father stood still, and listened: a third time it was blown. I forget the term used to express it, but it was the signal which, my father well knew, implied that the party was lost in the woods. In a few minutes more my father beheld a man on horseback, with a female seated on the crupper, enter the cleared space, and ride up to him. At first, my father called to mind the strange stories which he had heard of the supernatural beings who were said to frequent these mountains; but the nearer approach of the parties satisfied him that they were mortals like himself.

'As soon as they came up to him, the man who guided the horse accosted him. "Friend Hunter, you are out late, the better fortune for us: we have ridden far, and are in fear of our lives, which are eagerly sought after. These mountains have enabled us to elude our pursuers; but if we find not shelter and refreshment, that will avail us little, as we must perish from hunger and the inclemency of the night. My daughter, who rides behind me, is now more dead than alive, – say, can you assist us in our difficulty?"

' "My cottage is some few miles distant," replied my father, "but I have little to offer you besides a shelter from the weather; to the little I have you are welcome. May I ask whence you come?"

' "Yes, friend, it is no secret now; we have escaped from Transylvania, where my daughter's honour and my life were equally in jeopardy!"

'This information was quite enough to raise an interest in my father's heart. He remembered his own escape: he remembered the loss of his wife's honour, and the tragedy by which it was wound up. He immediately, and warmly, offered all the assistance which he could afford them.

' "There is no time to be lost, then, good sir," observed the horseman; "my daughter is chilled with the frost, and cannot hold out much longer against the severity of the weather."

' "Follow me," replied my father, leading the way towards his home. "I was lured away in pursuit of a large white wolf," observed my father; "it came to the very window of my hut, or I should not have been out at this time of night."

' "The creature passed by us just as we came out of the wood," said the female in a silvery tone.

' "I was nearly discharging my piece at it," observed the hunter; "but since it did us such good service, I am glad that I allowed it to escape."

'In about an hour and a half, during which my father walked at a rapid pace, the party arrived at the cottage, and, as I said before, came in.

' "We are in good time, apparently,' observed the dark hunter, catching the smell of the roasted meat, as he walked to the fire and surveyed my brother and sister, and myself. "You have young cooks here, Mynheer."

' "I am glad that we shall not have to wait," replied my father. "Come, mistress, seat yourself by the fire; you require warmth after your cold ride."

' "And where can I put up my horse, Mynheer?" observed the huntsman.'

' "I will take care of him," replied my father, going out of the cottage door.

'The female must, however, be particularly described. She was young, and apparently twenty years of age. She was dressed in a travelling dress, deeply bordered with white fur, and wore a cap of white ermine on her head. Her features were very beautiful, at least I thought so, and so my father has since declared. Her hair was flaxen, glossy and shining, and bright as a mirror; and her mouth, although somewhat large when it was open, showed the most brilliant teeth I have ever beheld. But there was something about her eyes, bright as they were, which made us children afraid; they were so restless, so furtive; I could not at that time tell why, but I felt as if there was cruelty in her eye; and when she beckoned us to come to her, we approached her with fear and trembling. Still she was beautiful, very beautiful. She spoke kindly to my brother and myself, patted our heads, and caressed us; but Marcella would not come near her; on the contrary, she slunk away, and hid herself in the bed, and would not wait for the supper, which half an hour before she had been so anxious for.

'My father, having put the horse into a close shed, soon returned, and supper was placed upon the table. When it was over, my father requested that the young lady would take possession of his bed, and he would remain at the fire, and sit up with her father. After some hesitation on her part, this arrangement was agreed to, and I and my brother crept into the other bed with Marcella, for we had as yet always slept together.

'But we could not sleep; there was something so unusual, not only in seeing strange people, but in having those people sleep at the cottage, that we were bewildered. As for poor little Marcella, she was quiet, but I perceived that she trembled during the whole night, and sometimes I thought that she was checking a sob. My father had brought out some spirits, which he rarely used, and he and the strange hunter remained drinking and talking before the fire. Our ears were ready to catch the slightest whisper – so much was our curiosity excited.

' "You said you came from Transylvania?" observed my father.

' "Even so, Mynheer," replied the hunter. "I was a serf to the noble house of — — ; my master would insist upon my surrendering up my fair girl to his wishes; it ended in my giving him a few inches of my hunting-knife."

' "We are countrymen, and brothers in misfortune," replied my father, taking the huntsman's hand, and pressing it warmly.

' "Indeed! Are you, then, from that country?"

' "Yes; and I too have fled for my life. But mine is a melancholy tale."

' "Your name?" inquired the hunter.

' "Krantz."

' "What! Krantz of — — ! I have heard your tale; you need not renew your grief by repeating it now. Welcome, most welcome, Mynheer, and, I may say, my worthy kinsman. I am your second cousin, Wilfred of Barnsdorf," cried the hunter, rising up and embracing my father.

'They filled their horn mugs to the brim, and drank to one another, after the German fashion. The conversation was then carried on in a low tone; all that we could collect from it was, that our new relative and his daughter were to take up their abode in our cottage, at least for the present. In about an hour they both fell back in their chairs, and appeared to sleep.

' "Marcella, dear, did you hear?" said my brother in a low tone.

' "Yes," replied Marcella, in a whisper; "I heard all. Oh! brother, I cannot bear to look upon that woman – I feel so frightened."

'My brother made no reply, and shortly afterwards we were all three fast asleep.

'When we awoke the next morning, we found that the hunter's daughter had risen before us. I thought she looked more beautiful than ever. She came up to little Marcella and caressed her; the child burst into tears, and sobbed as if her heart would break.

'But, not to detain you with too long a story, the huntsman and his daughter were accommodated in the cottage. My father and he went out hunting daily, leaving Christina with us. She performed all the household duties; was very kind to us children; and, gradually, the dislike even of little Marcella wore away. But a great change took place in my father; he appeared to have conquered his aversion to the sex, and was most attentive to Christina. Often, after her father and we were in bed, would he sit up with her, conversing in a low tone by the fire. I ought to have mentioned, that my father and the huntsman Wilfred, slept in another portion of the cottage, and that the bed which he formerly occupied, and which was in the same room as ours, had been given up to the use of Christina. These visitors had been about three weeks at the cottage, when, one night, after we children had been sent to bed, a consultation was held. My father had asked Christina in marriage, and had obtained both her own consent and that of Wilfred; after this a conversation took place, which was, as nearly as I can recollect, as follows –

' "You may take my child, Mynheer Krantz, and my blessing with her, and I shall then leave you and seek some other habitation – it matters little where."

' "Why not remain here, Wilfred?"

' "No, no, I am called elsewhere; let that suffice, and ask no more questions. You have my child."

' "I thank you for her, and will duly value her; but there is one difficulty."

' "I know what you would say; there is no priest here in this wild country: true; neither is there any law to bind; still must some ceremony pass between you, to satisfy a father. Will you consent to marry her after my fashion? if so, I will marry you directly."

' "I will," replied my father.

' "Then take her by the hand. Now, Mynheer, swear."

' "I swear," repeated my father.

' "By all the spirits of the Hartz Mountains – "

' "Nay, why not by Heaven?" interrupted my father.

' "Because it is not my humour," rejoined Wilfred; "if I prefer that oath, less binding perhaps, than another, surely you will not thwart me."

' "Well, be it so then; have your humour. Will you make me swear by that in which I do not believe?"

' "Yet many do so, who in outward appearance are Christians," rejoined Wilfred; "say, will you be married, or shall I take my daughter away with me?"

' "Proceed," replied my father, impatiently.

' "I swear by all the spirits of the Hartz Mountains, by all their power for good or for evil, that I take Christina for my wedded wife; that I will ever protect her, cherish her, and love her; that my hand shall never be raised against her to harm her."

'My father repeated the words after Wilfred.

' "And if I fail in this my vow, may all the vengeance of the spirits fall upon me and upon my children; may they perish by the vulture, by the wolf, or other beasts of the forest; may their flesh be torn from their limbs, and their bones blanch in the wilderness; all this I swear."

'My father hesitated, as he repeated the last words; little Marcella could not restrain herself, and as my father repeated the last sentence, she burst into tears. This sudden interruption appeared to discompose the party, particularly my father; he spoke harshly to the child, who controlled her sobs, burying her face under the bedclothes.

'Such was the second marriage of my father. The next morning, the hunter Wilfred mounted his horse, and rode away.

'My father resumed his bed, which was in the same room as ours; and things went on much as before the marriage, except that our new mother-in-law did not show any kindness towards us; indeed, during my father's absence, she would often beat us, particularly little Marcella, and her eyes would flash fire, as she looked eagerly upon the fair and lovely child.

'One night, my sister awoke me and my brother.

' "What is the matter?" said Caesar.

' "She has gone out," whispered Marcella.

' "Gone out!"

' "Yes, gone out at the door, in her night-clothes," replied the child; "I saw her get out of bed, look at my father to see if he slept, and then she went out at the door."

'What could induce her to leave her bed, and all undressed to go out, in such bitter wintry weather, with the snow deep on the ground, was to us incomprehensible; we lay awake, and in about an hour we heard the growl of a wolf, close under the window.

' "There is a wolf," said Caesar; "she will be torn to pieces."

' "Oh, no!" cried Marcella.

'In a few minutes afterwards our mother-in-law appeared; she was in her night-dress, as Marcella had stated. She let down the latch of the door, so as to make no noise, went to a pail of water, and washed her face and hands, and then slipped into the bed where my father lay.

'We all three trembled, we hardly knew why, but we resolved to watch the next night: we did so – and not only on the ensuing night, but on many others, and always at about the same hour, would our mother-in-law rise from her bed, and leave the cottage – and after she was gone, we invariably heard the growl of a wolf under our window, and always saw her, on her return, wash herself before she retired to bed. We observed, also, that she seldom sat down to meals, and that when she did, she appeared to eat with dislike; but when the meat was taken down, to be prepared for dinner, she would often furtively put a raw piece into her mouth.

'My brother Caesar was a courageous boy; he did not like to speak to my father until he knew more. He resolved that he would follow her out, and ascertain what she did. Marcella and I endeavoured to dissuade him from this project; but he would not be controlled, and the very next night he lay down in his clothes, and as soon as our mother-in-law had left the cottage, he jumped up, took down my father's gun, and followed her.

'You may imagine in what a state of suspense Marcella and I remained, during his absence. After a few minutes, we heard the report of a gun. It did not awaken my father, and we lay trembling with anxiety. In a minute afterwards we saw our mother-in-law enter the cottage – her dress was bloody. I put my hand to Marcella's mouth to prevent her crying out, although I was myself in great alarm. Our mother-in-law approached my father's bed, looked to see if he was asleep, and then went to the chimney, and blew up the embers into a blaze.

' "Who is there?" said my father, waking up.

' "Lie still, dearest," replied my mother-in-law, "it is only me; I have lighted the fire to warm some water; I am not quite well."

'My father turned round and was soon asleep; but we watched our mother-in-law. She changed her linen, and threw the garments she had worn into the fire; and we then perceived that her right leg was bleeding profusely, as if from a gunshot wound. She bandaged it up, and then dressing herself, remained before the fire until the break of day.

'Poor little Marcella, her heart beat quick as she pressed me to her side – so indeed did mine. Where was our brother, Caesar? How did my mother-in-law receive the wound unless from his gun? At last my father rose, and then, for the first time I spoke, saying,. "Father, where is my brother, Caesar?"

' "Your brother!" exclaimed he, "why, where can he be?"

' "Merciful Heaven! I thought as I lay very restless last night," observed our mother-in-law, "that I heard somebody open the latch of the door; and, dear me, husband, what has become of your gun?"

'My father cast his eyes up above the chimney, and perceived that his gun was missing. For a moment he looked perplexed, then seizing a broad axe, he went out of the cottage without saying another word.

'He did not remain away from us long: in a few minutes he returned, bearing in his arms the mangled body of my poor brother; he laid it down, and covered up his face.

'My mother-in-law rose up, and looked at the body, while Marcella and I threw ourselves by its side wailing and sobbing bitterly.

'"Go to bed again, children," said she sharply. "Husband," continued she, "your boy must have taken the gun down to shoot a wolf, and the animal has been too powerful for him. Poor boy! he has paid dearly for his rashness."

'My father made no reply; I wished to speak – to tell all – but Marcella, who perceived my intention, held me by the arm, and looked at me so imploringly, that I desisted.

'My father, therefore, was left in his error; but Marcella and I, although we could not comprehend it, were conscious that our mother-in-law was in some way connected with my brother's death.

'That day my father went out and dug a grave, and when he laid the body in the earth, he piled up stones over it, so that the wolves should not be able to dig it up. The shock of this catastrophe was to my poor father very severe; for several days he never went to the chase, although at times he would utter bitter anathemas and vengeance against the wolves.

'But during this time of mourning on his part, my mother-in-law's nocturnal wanderings continued with the same regularity as before.

'At last, my father took down his gun, to repair to the forest; but he soon returned, and appeared much annoyed.

'"Would you believe it, Christina, that the wolves – perdition to the whole race – have actually contrived to dig up the body of my poor boy, and now there is nothing left of him but his bones?"

'"Indeed!" replied my mother-in-law. Marcella looked at me, and I saw in her intelligent eye all she would have uttered.

'"A wolf growls under our window every night, father," said I.

'"Aye, indeed? – Why did you not tell me, boy? – Wake me the next time you hear it."

'I saw my mother-in-law turn away; her eyes flashed fire, and she gnashed her teeth.

'My father went out again, and covered up with a larger pile of stones the little remnants of my poor brother which the wolves had spared. Such was the first act of the tragedy.

'The spring now came on: the snow disappeared, and we were permitted to leave the cottage; but never would I quit, for one moment, my dear little sister, to whom, since the death of my brother,

I was more ardently attached than ever; indeed I was afraid to leave her alone with my mother-in-law, who appeared to have a particular pleasure in ill-treating the child. My father was now employed upon his little farm, and I was able to render him some assistance.

'Marcella used to sit by us while we were at work, leaving my mother-in-law alone in the cottage. I ought to observe that, as the spring advanced, so did my mother-in-law decrease her nocturnal rambles, and that we never heard the growl of the wolf under the window after I had spoken of it to my father.

'One day, when my father and I were in the field, Marcella being with us, my mother-in-law came out, saying that she was going into the forest to collect some herbs my father wanted, and that Marcella must go to the cottage and watch the dinner. Marcella went, and my mother-in-law soon disappeared in the forest, taking a direction quite contrary to that in which the cottage stood, and leaving my father and I, as it were, between her and Marcella.

'About an hour afterwards we were startled by shrieks from the cottage, evidently the shrieks of little Marcella. "Marcella has burnt herself, father," said I, throwing down my spade. My father threw down his, and we both hastened to the cottage. Before we could gain the door, out darted a large white wolf, which fled with the utmost celerity. My father had no weapon; he rushed into the cottage, and there saw poor little Marcella expiring: her body was dreadfully mangled, and the blood pouring from it had formed a large pool on the cottage floor. My father's first intention had been to seize his gun and pursue, but he was checked by this horrid spectacle; he knelt down by his dying child, and burst into tears: Marcella could just look kindly on us for a few seconds, and then her eyes were closed in death.

'My father and I were still hanging over my poor sister's body, when my mother-in-law came in. At the dreadful sight she expressed much concern, but she did not appear to recoil from the sight of blood, as most women do.

'"Poor child!' said she, 'it must have been that great white wolf which passed me just now, and frightened me so – she's quite dead, Krantz."

'"I know it – I know it!" cried my father in agony.

'I thought my father would never recover from the effects of this second tragedy: he mourned bitterly over the body of his sweet child, and for several days would not consign it to its grave, although frequently requested by my mother-in-law to do so. At last he yielded, and dug a grave for her close by that of my poor brother, and took every precaution that the wolves should not violate her remains.

'I was now really miserable, as I lay alone in the bed which I had formerly shared with my brother and sister. I could not help thinking that my mother-in-law was implicated in both their deaths, although I could not account for the manner; but I no longer felt afraid of her: my little heart was full of hatred and revenge.

'The night after my sister had been buried, as I lay awake, I perceived my mother-in-law get up and go out of the cottage. I waited some time, then dressed myself, and looked out through the door, which I half opened. The moon shone bright, and I could see the spot where my brother and my sister had been buried; and what was my horror, when I perceived my mother-in-law busily removing the stones from Marcella's grave.

'She was in her white night-dress, and the moon shone full upon her. She was digging with her hands, and throwing away the stones behind her with all the ferocity of a wild beast. It was some time before I could collect my senses and decide what I should do. At last, I perceived that she had arrived at the body, and raised it up to the side of the grave. I could bear it no longer; I ran to my father and awoke him.

'"Father! father!" cried I, "dress yourself, and get your gun."

'"What!" cried my father, "the wolves are there, are they?"

'He jumped out of bed, threw on his clothes, and in his anxiety did not appear to perceive the absence of his wife. As soon as he was ready, I opened the door, he went out, and I followed him.

'Imagine his horror, when (unprepared as he was for such a sight) he beheld, as he advanced towards the grave, not a wolf, but his wife, in her night-dress, on her hands and knees, crouching by the body of my sister, and tearing off large pieces of the flesh, and devouring them with all the avidity of a wolf. She was too busy to be aware of our approach. My father dropped his gun, his hair stood on end; so did mine; he breathed heavily, and then his breath for a time stopped. I picked up the gun and put it into his hand. Suddenly he appeared as if concentrated rage had restored him to double vigour; he levelled his piece, fired, and with a loud shriek, down fell the wretch whom he had fostered in his bosom.

'"God of Heaven!" cried my father, sinking down upon the earth in a swoon, as soon as he had discharged his gun.

'I remained some time by his side before he recovered. "Where am I?" said he. "What has happened? – Oh! – yes, yes! I recollect now. Heaven forgive me!"

'He rose and we walked up to the grave; what again was our astonishment and horror to find that instead of the dead body of my mother-in-law, as we expected, there was lying over the remains of my poor sister, a large, white she-wolf.

' "The white wolf!" exclaimed my father, "the white wolf which decoyed me into the forest – I see it all now – I have dealt with the spirits of the Hartz Mountains."

'For some time my father remained in silence and deep thought. He then carefully lifted up the body of my sister, replaced it in the grave, and covered it over as before, having struck the head of the dead animal with the heel of his boot, and raving like a madman. He walked back to the cottage, shut the door, and threw himself on the bed; I did the same, for I was in a stupor of amazement.

'Early in the morning we were both roused by a loud knocking at the door, and in rushed the hunter Wilfred.

' "My daughter! – Man – my daughter! – where is my daughter!" cried he in a rage.

' "Where the wretch, the fiend, should be, I trust," replied my father, starting up and displaying equal choler; "where she should be – in hell! – Leave this cottage or you may fare worse."

' "Ha – ha!" replied the hunter, "would you harm a potent spirit of the Hartz Mountains. Poor mortal, who must needs wed a weir wolf."

' "Out demon! I defy thee and thy power."

' "Yet shall you feel it; remember your oath – your solemn oath – never to raise your hand against her to harm her."

' "I made no compact with evil spirits."

' "You did; and if you failed in your vow, you were to meet the vengeance of the spirits. Your children were to perish by the vulture, the wolf – "

' "Out, out, demon!"

' "And their bones blanch in the wilderness. Ha! – ha!"

'My father, frantic with rage, seized his axe, and raised it over Wilfred's head to strike.

' "All this I swear," continued the huntsman, mockingly.

'The axe descended; but it passed through the form of the hunter, and my father lost his balance, and fell heavily on the floor.

' "Mortal!" said the hunter, striding over my father's body, "we have power over those only who have committed murder. You have been guilty of a double murder – you shall pay the penalty attached to your marriage vow. Two of your children are gone; the third is yet to follow – and follow them he will, for your oath is registered. Go – it were kindness to kill thee – your punishment is – that you live!"

'With these words the spirit disappeared. My father rose from the floor, embraced me tenderly, and knelt down in prayer.

'The next morning he quitted the cottage for ever. He took me with him and bent his steps to Holland, where we safely arrived. He had some little money with him; but he had not been many days in Amsterdam before he was seized with a brain fever, and died raving mad. I was put into the Asylum, and afterwards was sent to sea before the mast. You now know all my history. The question is, whether I am to pay the penalty of my father's oath? I am myself perfectly convinced that, in some way or another, I shall.'

On the twenty-second day the high land of the south of Sumatra was in view; as there were no vessels in sight, they resolved to keep their course through the Straits, and run for Pulo Penang, which they expected, as their vessel laid so close to the wind, to reach in seven or eight days. By constant exposure, Philip and Krantz were now so bronzed, that with their long beards and Mussulman dresses, they might easily have passed off for natives. They had steered during the whole of the days exposed to a burning sun; they had lain down and slept in the dew of night, but their health had not suffered. But for several days, since he had confided the history of his family to Philip, Krantz had become silent and melancholy; his usual flow of spirits had vanished, and Philip had often questioned him as to the cause. As they entered the Straits, Philip talked of what they should do upon their arrival at Goa, when Krantz gravely replied, 'For some days, Philip, I have had a presentiment that I shall never see that city.'

'You are out of health, Krantz,' replied Philip.

'No; I am in sound health, body and mind. I have endeavoured to shake off the presentiment, but in vain; there is a warning voice that continually tells me that I shall not be long with you. Philip, will you oblige me by making me content on one point: I have gold about my person which may be useful to you; oblige me by taking it, and securing it on your own.'

'What nonsense, Krantz.'

'It is no nonsense, Philip. Have you not had your warnings? Why should I not have mine? You know that I have little fear in my composition, and that I care not about death; but I feel the presentiment which I speak of more strongly every hour. It is some kind spirit who would warn me to prepare for another world. Be it so.

I have lived long enough in this world to leave it without regret; although to part with you and Amine, the only two now dear to me, is painful, I acknowledge.'

'May not this arise from over-exertion and fatigue, Krantz? Consider how much excitement you have laboured under within these last four months. Is not that enough to create a corresponding depression? Depend upon it, my dear friend, such is the fact.'

'I wish it were – but I feel otherwise, and there is a feeling of gladness connected with the idea that I am to leave this world, arising from another presentiment, which equally occupies my mind.'

'Which is?'

'I hardly can tell you; but Amine and you are connected with it. In my dreams I have seen you meet again; but it has appeared to me, as if a portion of your trial was purposely shut from my sight in dark clouds; and I have asked, "May not I see what is there concealed?" – and an invisible has answered, "No! 'twould make you wretched. Before these trials take place, you will be summoned away" – and then I have thanked Heaven, and felt resigned.'

'These are the imaginings of a disturbed brain, Krantz; that I am destined to suffering may be true; but why Amine should suffer, or why you, young, in full health and vigour, should not pass your days in peace, and live to a good old age, there is no cause for believing. You will be better tomorrow.'

'Perhaps so,' replied Krantz; – 'but still you must yield to my whim, and take the gold. If I am wrong, and we do arrive safe, you know, Philip, you can let me have it back,' observed Krantz, with a faint smile – 'but you forget, our water is nearly out, and we must look out for a rill on the coast to obtain a fresh supply.'

'I was thinking of that when you commenced this unwelcome topic. We had better look out for the water before dark, and as soon as we have replenished our jars, we will make sail again.'

At the time that this conversation took place, they were on the eastern side of the Strait, about forty miles to the northward. The interior of the coast was rocky and mountainous, but it slowly descended to low land of alternate forest and jungles, which continued to the beach: the country appeared to be uninhabited. Keeping close in to the shore, they discovered, after two hours' run, a fresh stream which burst in a cascade from the mountains, and swept its devious course through the jungle, until it poured its tribute into the waters of the Strait.

They ran close in to the mouth of the stream, lowered the sails, and pulled the peroqua against the current, until they had advanced far enough to assure them that the water was quite fresh. The jars were soon filled, and they were again thinking of pushing off; when, enticed by the beauty of the spot, the coolness of the fresh water, and wearied with their long confinement on board of the peroqua, they proposed to bathe – a luxury hardly to be appreciated by those who have not been in a similar situation. They threw off their Mussulman dresses, and plunged into the stream, where they remained for some time. Krantz was the first to get out; he complained of feeling chilled, and he walked on to the banks where their clothes had been laid. Philip also approached nearer to the beach, intending to follow him.

'And now, Philip,' said Krantz, 'this will be a good opportunity for me to give you the money. I will open my sash, and pour it out, and you can put it into your own before you put it on.'

Philip was standing in the water, which was about level with his waist.

'Well, Krantz,' said he, 'I suppose if it must be so, it must; but it appears to me an idea so ridiculous – however, you shall have your own way.'

Philip quitted the run, and sat down by Krantz, who was already busy in shaking the doubloons out of the folds of his sash; at last he said – 'I believe, Philip, you have got them all, now? – I feel satisfied.'

'What danger there can be to you, which I am not equally exposed to, I cannot conceive,' replied Philip; 'however – '

Hardly had he said these words, when there was a tremendous roar – a rush like a mighty wind through the air – a blow which threw him on his back – a loud cry – and a contention. Philip recovered himself, and perceived the naked form of Krantz carried off with the speed of an arrow by an enormous tiger through the jungle. He watched with distended eyeballs; in a few seconds the animal and Krantz had disappeared!

'God of Heaven! Would that Thou hadst spared me this,' cried Philip, throwing himself down in agony on his face. 'Oh! Krantz, my friend – my brother – too sure was your presentiment. Merciful God! have pity – but Thy will be done;' and Philip burst into a flood of tears.

For more than an hour did he remain fixed upon the spot, careless and indifferent to the danger by which he was surrounded. At last, somewhat recovered, he rose, dressed himself, and then again sat down – his eyes fixed upon the clothes of Krantz, and the gold which still lay on the sand.

'He would give me that gold. He foretold his doom. Yes! yes! it was his destiny, and it has been fulfilled. *His bones will bleach in the wilderness*, and the spirit-hunter and his wolfish daughter are avenged.'

The White Wolf of Kostopchin

SIR GILBERT CAMPBELL

A wide sandy expanse of country, flat and uninteresting in appearance, with a great staring whitewashed house standing in the midst of wide fields of cultivated land, whilst far away were the low sandhills and pine forests to be met with in the district of Lithuania, in Russian Poland. Not far from the great white house was the village in which the serfs dwelt, with the large bakehouse and the public bath which are invariably to be found in all Russian villages, however humble. The fields were negligently cultivated, the hedges broken down and the fences in bad repair; shattered agricultural implements had been carelessly flung aside in remote corners, and the whole estate showed the want of the superintending eye of an energetic master. The great white house was no better looked after, the garden was an utter wilderness, great patches of plaster had fallen from the walls, and many of the Venetian shutters were almost off the hinges. Over all was the dark lowering sky of a Russian autumn, and there were no signs of life to be seen, save a few peasants lounging idly towards the vodka shop, and a gaunt halt-starved cat creeping stealthily abroad in quest of a meal.

The estate, which was known by the name of Kostopchin, was the property of Paul Sergevitch, a gentleman of means, and the most discontented man in Russian Poland. Like most wealthy Muscovites, he had travelled much, and had spent the gold which had been amassed by serf labour, like water, in all the dissolute revelries of the capitals of Europe. Paul's figure was as well known in the boudoirs of the *demi-mondaines* as his face was familiar at the public gaming tables. He appeared to have no thought for the future, but only to live in the excitement of the mad career of dissipation which he was pursuing. His means, enormous as they were, were all forestalled, and he was continually sending to his intendant for fresh supplies of money. His fortune would not have long held out against the constant inroads that were being made upon it, when an unexpected circumstance took place which stopped his career like a flash of lightning. This was a fatal duel, in which a young man of great promise, the son of the prime minister of the country in which he then resided, fell by his hand. Representations were made to the Tsar, and Paul Sergevitch was recalled, and, after receiving a severe reprimand was ordered to return to his estates in Lithuania. Horribly discontented, yet not daring to disobey the Imperial mandate, Paul buried himself at Kostopchin, a place he had not visited since his boyhood. At first he endeavoured to interest himself in the workings of the vast estate; but agriculture had no charm for him, and the only result was that he quarrelled with and dismissed his German intendant, replacing him by an old serf, Michal Vassilitch, who had been his father's valet. Then he took to wandering about the country, gun in hand, and upon his return home would sit moodily drinking brandy and smoking innumerable cigarettes, as he cursed his lord and master, the emperor, for consigning him to such a course of dullness and ennui. For a couple of years he led this aimless life, and at last, hardly knowing the reason for so doing, he married the daughter of a neighbouring landed proprietor. The marriage was a most unhappy one; the girl had really never cared for Paul, but had married him in obedience to her father's mandates, and the man, whose temper was always brutal and violent, treated her, after a brief interval of contemptuous indifference, with savage cruelty. After three years the unhappy woman expired, leaving behind her two children – a boy, Alexis, and a girl, Katrina. Paul treated his wife's death with the most perfect indifference; but he did not put anyone in her place. He was very fond of the little Katrina, but did not take much notice of the boy, and resumed his lonely wanderings about the country with dog and gun. Five years had passed since the death of his wife. Alexis was a fine, healthy boy of seven, whilst Katrina was some eighteen months younger. Paul was lighting one of his eternal cigarettes at the door of his house, when the little girl came running up to him.

'You bad, wicked papa,' said she. 'How is it that you have never brought me the pretty grey squirrels that you promised I should have the next time you went to the forest?'

'Because I have never yet been able to find any, my treasure,' returned her father, taking up his child in his arms and half smothering her with kisses. 'Because I have not found them yet, my golden queen; but I am bound to find Ivanovitch, the poacher, smoking about the woods, and if he can't show me where they are, no-one can.'

'Ah, little father,' broke in old Michal, using the term of address with which a Russian of humble position usually accosts his superior; 'Ah, little father, take care; you will go to those woods once too often.'

'Do you think I am afraid of Ivanovitch?' returned his master, with a coarse laugh. 'Why, he and I are the best of friends; at any rate, if he robs me, he does so openly, and keeps other poachers away from my woods.'

'It is not of Ivanovitch that I am thinking,' answered the old man. 'But oh! Gospodin, do not go into these dark solitudes; there are terrible tales told about them, of witches that dance in the moonlight, of strange, shadowy forms that are seen amongst the trunks of the tall pines, and of whispered voices that tempt the listeners to eternal perdition.'

Again the rude laugh of the lord of the manor rang out, as Paul observed, 'If you go on addling your brain, old man, with these nearly half-forgotten legends, I shall have to look out for a new intendant.'

'But I was not thinking of these fearful creatures only,' returned Michal, crossing himself piously. 'It was against the wolves that I meant to warn you.'

'Oh, father, dear, I am frightened now,' whimpered little Katrina, hiding her head on her father's shoulder. 'Wolves are such cruel, wicked things.'

'See there, greybearded dotard,' cried Paul, furiously, 'you have terrified this sweet angel by your farrago of lies; besides, who ever heard of wolves so early as this? You are dreaming, Michal Vassilitch, or have taken your morning dram of vodka too strong.'

'As I hope for future happiness,' answered the old man, solemnly, 'as I came through the marsh last night from Kosma the herdsman's cottage – you know, my lord, that he has been bitten by a viper, and is seriously ill – as I came through the marsh, I repeat, I saw something like sparks of fire in the clump of alders on the right-hand side. I was anxious to know what they could be, and cautiously moved a little nearer, recommending my soul to the protection of Saint Vladimir. I had not gone a couple of paces when a wild howl came that chilled the very marrow of my bones, and a pack of some ten or a dozen wolves, gaunt and famished as you see them, my lord, in the winter, rushed out. At their head was a white she-wolf, as big as any of the male ones, with gleaming tusks and a pair of yellow eyes that blazed with lurid fire. I had round my neck a crucifix that had been given me by the priest of Streletza, and the savage beasts knew this and broke away across the marsh, sending up the mud and water in showers in the air; but the white she-wolf, little father, circled round me three times, as though endeavouring to find some place from which to attack me. Three times she did this, and then, with a snap of her teeth and a howl of impotent malice, she galloped away some fifty yards and sat down, watching my every movement with her fiery eyes. I did not delay any longer in so dangerous a spot, as you may well imagine, Gospodin, but walked hurriedly home, crossing myself at every step; but, as I am a living man, that white devil followed me the whole distance, keeping fifty paces in the rear, and every now and then licking her lips with a sound that made my flesh creep. When I got to the last fence before you come to the house I raised up my voice and shouted for the dogs, and soon I heard the deep bay of Troska and Branskoe as they came bounding towards me. The white devil heard it, too, and, giving a high bound into the air, she uttered a loud howl of disappointment, and trotted back leisurely towards the marsh.'

'But why did you not set the dogs after her?' asked Paul, interested, in spite of himself, at the old man's narrative. 'In the open Troska and Branskoe would run down any wolf that ever set foot to the ground in Lithuania.'

'I tried to do so, little father,' answered the old man, solemnly; 'but directly they got up to the spot where the beast had executed her last devilish gambol, they put their tails between their legs and ran back to the house as fast as their legs could carry them.'

'Strange,' muttered Paul, thoughtfully. 'That is, if it is truth and not vodka that is speaking.'

'My lord,' returned the old man, reproachfully, 'man and boy, I have served you and my lord your father for fifty years, and no-one can say that they ever saw Michal Vassilitch the worse for liquor.'

'No-one doubts that you are a sly old thief, Michal,' returned his master, with his coarse, jarring laugh; 'but for all that, your long stories of having been followed by white wolves won't prevent me from going to the forest today. A couple of good buckshot cartridges will break any spell, though I don't think that the she-wolf, if she existed any-where other than in your own imagination, has anything to do with magic. Don't be frightened, Katrina, my pet; you shall have a fine white wolf skin to put your feet on, if what this old fool says is right.'

'Michal is not a fool,' pouted the child, 'and it is very wicked of you to call him so. I don't want any nasty wolf skins, I want the grey squirrels.' .

And you shall have them, my precious,' returned her father, setting her down upon the ground. 'Be a good girl, and I will not be long away.'

'Father,' said the little Alexis, suddenly, 'let me go with you. I should like to see you kill a wolf, and then I should know how to do so, when I grow older and taller.'

'Pshaw,' returned his father, irritably. 'Boys are always in the way. Take the lad away, Michal; don't you see that he is worrying his sweet little sister?'

'No, no, he does not worry me at all,' answered the impetuous little lady, as she flew to her brother and covered him with kisses. 'Michal, you shan't take him away, do you hear?'

'There, there, leave the children together,' returned Paul, as he shouldered his gun, and kissing the tips of his fingers to Katrina, stepped away rapidly in the direction of the dark pine woods. Paul walked on, humming the fragment of an air that he had heard in a very different place many years ago. A strange feeling of elation crept over him, very different to the false excitement which his solitary drinking bouts were wont to produce. A change seemed to have come over his whole life, the skies looked brighter, the spiculae of the pine trees of a more vivid green, and the landscape seemed to have lost that dull cloud of depression which had for years appeared to hang over it. And beneath all this exaltation of the mind, beneath all this unlooked-for promise of a more happy future, lurked a heavy, inexplicable feeling of a power to come, a something without form or shape, and yet the more terrible because it was shrouded by that thick veil which conceals from the eyes of the soul the strange fantastic designs of the dwellers beyond the line of earthly influences.

There were no signs of the poacher, and wearied with searching for him, Paul made the woods reëcho with his name. The great dog, Troska, which had followed his master, looked up wistfully into his face, and at a second repetition of the name 'Ivanovitch', uttered a long plaintive howl, and then, looking round at Paul as though entreating him to follow, moved slowly ahead towards a denser portion of the forest. A little mystified at the hound's unusual proceedings, Paul followed, keeping his gun ready to fire at the least sign of danger. He thought that he knew the forest well, but the dog led the way to a portion which he never remembered to have visited before. He had got away from the pine trees now, and had entered a dense thicket formed of stunted oaks and hollies. The great dog kept only a yard or so ahead; his lips were drawn back, showing the strong white fangs, the hair upon his neck and back was bristling, and his tail firmly pressed between his hind legs. Evidently the animal was in a state of the most extreme terror, and yet it proceeded bravely forward. Struggling through the dense thicket, Paul suddenly found himself in an open space of some ten or twenty yards in diameter. At one end of it was a slimy pool, into the waters of which several strange-looking reptiles glided as the man and dog made their appearance. Almost in the centre of the opening was a shattered stone cross, and at its base lay a dark heap, close to which Troska stopped, and again raising his head, uttered a long melancholy howl. For an instant or two, Paul gazed hesitatingly at the shapeless heap that lay beneath the cross, and then, mustering up all his courage, he stepped forwards and bent anxiously over it. Once glance was enough, for he recognised the body of Ivanovitch the poacher, hideously mangled. With a cry of surprise, he turned over the body and shuddered as he gazed upon the terrible injuries that had been inflicted. The unfortunate man had evidently been attacked by some savage beast, for there were marks of teeth upon the throat, and the jugular vein had been almost torn out. The breast of the corpse had been torn open, evidently by long sharp claws, and there was a gaping orifice upon the left side, round which the blood had formed in a thick coagulated patch. The only animals to be found in the forests of Russia capable of inflicting such wounds are the bear or the wolf, and the question as to the class of the assailant was easily settled by a glance at the dank ground, which showed the prints of a wolf so entirely different from the plantigrade traces of the bear.

'Savage brutes,' muttered Paul. 'So, after all, there may have been some truth in Michal's story, and the old idiot may for once in his life have spoken the truth. Well, it is no concern of mine, and if a fellow chooses to wander about the woods at night to kill my game, instead of remaining in his own hovel, he must take his chance. The strange thing is that the brutes have not eaten him, though they have mauled him so terribly.'

He turned away as he spoke, intending to return home and send out some of the serfs to bring in the body of the unhappy man, when his eye was caught by a small white object, hanging from a bramble bush near the pond. He made towards the spot, and taking up the object, examined it curiously. It was a tuft of coarse white hair, evidently belonging to some animal.'

'A wolf's hair, or I am much mistaken,' muttered Paul, pressing the hair between his fingers, and then applying it to his nose. 'And from its colour, I should think that it belonged to the white lady who so terribly alarmed old Michal on the occasion of his night walk through the marsh.'

Paul found it no easy task to retrace his steps towards those parts of the forest with which he was acquainted, and Troska seemed unable to render him the slightest assistance, but followed moodily behind. Many times Paul found his way blocked by impenetrable thicket or dangerous quagmire, and during his many wanderings he had the ever-present sensation that there was a something close to him, an invisible something, a noiseless something, but for all that a presence which moved as he advanced, and halted as he stopped in vain to listen. The certainty that an impalpable thing of some shape or other was close at hand grew so strong, that as the short autumn day began to close, and darker shadows to fall between the trunks of the lofty trees, it made him hurry on at his utmost speed. At length, when he had grown almost mad with terror, he suddenly came upon a path he knew, and with a feeling of intense relief, he stepped briskly forward in the direction of Kostopchin. As he left the forest and came into the open country, a faint wail seemed to ring through the darkness; but Paul's nerves had been so much shaken that he did not know whether this was an actual fact or only the offspring of his own excited fancy. As he crossed the neglected lawn that lay in front of the house, old Michal came rushing out of the house with terror convulsing every feature.

'Oh, my lord, my lord!' gasped he, 'is not this too terrible?'

'Nothing has happened to my Katrina?' cried the father, a sudden sickly feeling of terror passing through his heart.

'No, no, the little lady is quite safe, thanks to the Blessed Virgin and Saint Alexander of Nevskoi,' returned Michal; 'but oh, my lord, poor Marta, the herd's daughter – '

'Well, what of the slut?' demanded Paul, for now that his momentary fear for the safety of his daughter had passed away, he had but little sympathy to spare for so insignificant a creature as a serf girl.

'I told you that Kosma was dying,' answered Michal. 'Well, Marta went across the marsh this afternoon to fetch the priest, but alas! she never came back.'

'What detained her, then?' asked his master.

'One of the neighbours, going in to see how Kosma was getting on, found the poor old man dead; his face was terribly contorted, and he was half in the bed, and half out, as though he had striven to reach the door. The man ran to the village to give the alarm, and as the men returned to the herdsman's hut, they found the body of Marta in a thicket by the clump of alders on the marsh.'

'Her body – she was dead then?' asked Paul.

'Dead, my lord; killed by wolves,' answered the old man. 'And oh, my lord, it is too horrible, her breast was horribly lacerated, and her heart had been taken out and eaten, for it was nowhere to be found.'

Paul started, for the horrible mutilation of the body of Ivanovitch the poacher occurred to his recollection.

'And, my lord,' continued the old man, 'this is not all; on a bush close by was this tuft of hair,' and, as he spoke, he took it from a piece of paper in which it was wrapped and handed it to his master.

Paul took it and recognised a similar tuft of hair to that which he had seen upon the bramble bush beside the shattered cross.

'Surely, my lord,' continued Michal, not heeding his master's look of surprise, 'you will have out men and dogs to hunt down this terrible creature, or, better still, send for the priest and holy water, for I have my doubts whether the creature belongs to this earth.'

Paul shuddered, and, after a short pause, he told Michal of the ghastly end of Ivanovitch the poacher.

The old man listened with the utmost excitement, crossing himself repeatedly, and muttering invocations to the Blessed Virgin and the saints every instant; but his master would no longer listen to him, and, ordering him to place brandy on the table, sat drinking moodily until daylight.

The next day a fresh horror awaited the inhabitants of Kostopchin. An old man, a confirmed drunkard, had staggered out of the vodka shop with the intention of returning home; three hours later he was found at a turn of the road, horribly scratched and mutilated, with the same gaping orifice in the left side of the breast, from which the heart had been forcibly torn out.

Three several times in the course of the week the same ghastly tragedy occurred – a little child, an able-bodied labourer, and an old woman, were all found with the same terrible marks of mutilation upon them, and in every case the same tuft of white hair was found in the immediate vicinity of the bodies. A frightful panic ensued, and an excited crowd of serfs surrounded the house at Kostopchin, calling upon their master, Paul Sergevitch, to save them from the fiend that had been let loose upon them, and shouting out various remedies, which they insisted upon being carried into effect at once.

Paul felt a strange disinclination to adopt any active measures. A certain feeling which he could not account for urged him to remain quiescent; but the Russian serf when suffering under an access of superstitious terror is a dangerous person to deal with, and, with extreme reluctance, Paul Sergevitch issued instructions for a thorough search through the estate, and a general *battue* of the pine woods.

The army of beaters convened by Michal was ready with the first dawn of sunrise, and formed a strange and almost grotesque-looking assemblage, armed with rusty old firelocks, heavy bludgeons, and scythes fastened on to the end of long poles. Paul, with his double-barrelled gun thrown across his shoulder and a keen hunting knife thrust into his belt, marched at the head of the serfs, accompanied by the two great hounds, Troska and Bransköe. Every nook and corner of the hedgerows were examined, and the little outlying clumps were thoroughly searched, but without success; and at last a circle was formed round the larger portion of the forest, and with loud shouts, blowing of horns, and beating of copper cooking utensils, the crowd of eager serfs pushed their way through the brushwood. Frightened birds flew up, whirring through the pine branches; hares and rabbits darted from their hiding places behind tufts and hummocks of grass, and scurried away in the utmost terror. Occasionally a roe deer rushed through the thicket, or a wild boar burst through the thin lines of beaters, but no signs of wolves were to be seen. The circle grew narrower and yet more narrow, when all at once a wild shriek and a confused murmur of voices echoed through the pine trees. All rushed to the spot, and a young lad was discovered weltering in his blood and terribly mutilated, though life still lingered in the mangled frame. A few drops of vodka were poured down the throat, and he managed to gasp out that the white wolf had sprung upon him suddenly, and, throwing him to the ground, had commenced tearing at the flesh over his heart. He would inevitably have been killed, had not the animal quitted him, alarmed by the approach of the other beaters.

'The beast ran into that thicket,' gasped the boy, and then once more relapsed into a state on insensibility.

But the words of the wounded boy had been eagerly passed round, and a hundred different propositions were made.

'Set fire to the thicket,' exclaimed one.

'Fire a volley into it,' suggested another.

'A bold dash in, and trample the beast's life out,' shouted a third.

The first proposal was agreed to, and a hundred eager hands collected dried sticks and leaves, and then a light was kindled. Just as the fire was about to be applied, a soft, sweet voice issued from the centre of the thicket.

'Do not set fire to the forest, my dear friends; give me time to come out. Is it not enough for me to have been frightened to death by that awful creature?'

All started back in amazement, and Paul felt a strange, sudden thrill pass through his heart as those soft musical accents fell upon his ear.

There was a light rustling in the brushwood, and then a vision suddenly appeared, which filled the souls of the beholders with surprise. As the bushes divided, a fair woman, wrapped in a mantle of soft white fur, with a fantastically shaped travelling cap of green velvet upon her head, stood before them. She was exquisitely fair, and her long Titian red hair hung in dishevelled masses over her shoulders.

'My good man,' began she, with a certain tinge of aristocratic hauteur in her voice, 'is your master here?'

As moved by a spring, Paul stepped forward and mechanically raised his cap.

'I am Paul Sergevitch,' said he, 'and these woods are on my estate of Kostopchin. A fearful wolf has been committing a series of terrible devastations upon my people, and we have been endeavouring to hunt it down. A boy whom he has just wounded says that he ran into the thicket from which you have just emerged, to the surprise of us all.'

'I know,' answered the lady, fixing her clear, steel-blue eyes keenly upon Paul's face. 'The terrible beast rushed past me, and dived into a large cavity in the earth in the very centre of the thicket. It was a huge white wolf, and I greatly feared that it would devour me.'

'Ho, my men,' cried Paul, 'take spade and mattock, and dig out the monster, for she has come to the end of her tether at last. Madam, I do not know what chance has conducted you to this wild solitude, but the hospitality of Kostopchin is at your disposal, and I will, with your permission, conduct you there as soon as this scourge of the countryside has been dispatched.'

He offered his hand with some remains of his former courtesy, but started back with an expression of horror on his face.

'Blood,' cried he; 'why, madam, your hand and fingers are stained with blood.'

A faint colour rose to the lady's cheek, but it died away in an instant as she answered, with a faint smile: 'The dreadful creature was all covered with blood, and I suppose I must have stained my hands against the bushes through which it had passed, when I parted them in order to escape from the fiery death with which you threatened me.'

There was a ring of suppressed irony in her voice, and Paul felt his eyes drop before the glance of those cold steel-blue eyes. Meanwhile, urged to the utmost exertion by their fears, the serfs plied spade and mattock with the utmost vigour. The cavity was speedily enlarged, but, when a depth of eight feet had been attained, it was found to terminate in a little burrow not large enough to admit a rabbit, much less a creature of the white wolf's size. There were none of the tufts of white hair which had hitherto been always found beside the bodies of the victims, nor did that peculiar rank odour which always indicates the presence of wild animals hang about the spot.

The superstitious Muscovites crossed themselves, and scrambled out of the hole with grotesque alacrity. The mysterious disappearance of the monster which had committed such frightful ravages had cast a chill over the hearts of the ignorant peasants, and, unheeding the shouts of their master, they left the forest, which seemed to be overcast with the gloom of some impending calamity.

'Forgive the ignorance of these boors, madam,' said Paul, when he found himself alone with the strange lady, 'and permit me to escort you to my poor house, for you must have need of rest and refreshment, and – '

Here Paul checked himself abruptly, and a dark flush of embarrassment passed over his face.

'And,' said the lady, with the same faint smile, 'and you are dying with curiosity to know how I suddenly made my appearance from a thicket in your forest. You say that you are the lord of Kostopchin; then you are Paul Sergevitch, and should surely know how the ruler of Holy Russia takes upon himself to interfere with the doings of his children?'

'You know me, then?' exclaimed Paul, in some surprise.

'Yes, I have lived in foreign lands, as you have, and have heard your name often. Did you not break the bank at Blankburg? Did you not carry off Isola Menuti, the dancer, from a host of competitors; and, as a last instance of my knowledge, shall I recall to your memory a certain morning, on a sandy shore, with two men facing each other pistol in hand, the one young, fair, and boyish-looking, hardly twenty-two years of age, the other – '

'Hush!' exclaimed Paul, hoarsely; 'you evidently know me, but who in the fiend's name are you?'

'Simply a woman who once moved in society and read the papers, and who is now a hunted fugitive.'

'A fugitive!' returned Paul, hotly; 'who dares to persecute you?'

The lady moved a little closer to him, and then whispered in his ear: 'The police!'

'The police!' repeated Paul, stepping back a pace or two. 'The police!'

'Yes, Paul Sergevitch, the police,' returned the lady, 'that body at the mention of which it is said the very Emperor trembles as he sits in his gilded chambers in the Winter Palace. Yes, I have had the imprudence to speak my mind too freely, and – well, you know what women have to dread who fall into the hands of the police in Holy Russia. To avoid such infamous degradations I fled, accompanied by a faithful domestic. I fled in hopes of gaining the frontier, but a few versts from here a body of mounted police rode up. My poor old servant had the imprudence to resist, and was shot dead. Half wild with terror I fled into the forest, and wandered about until I heard the noise your serfs made in the beating of the woods. I thought it was the police, who had organised a search for me, and I crept into the thicket for the purpose of concealment. The rest you know. And now, Paul Sergevitch, tell me whether you dare give shelter to a proscribed fugitive such as I am.'

'Madam,' returned Paul, gazing into the clear-cut features before him, glowing with the animation of the recital, 'Kostopchin is ever open to misfortune – and beauty,' added he, with a bow.

'Ah!' cried the lady, with a laugh in which there was something sinister; 'I expect that misfortune would knock at your door for a long time, if it was unaccompanied by beauty. However, I thank you, and will accept your hospitality; but if evil come upon you, remember that I am not to be blamed.'

'You will be safe enough at Kostopchin,' returned Paul. 'The police won't trouble their heads about me; they know that since the Emperor drove me to lead this hideous existence, politics have no charm for me, and that the brandy bottle is the only charm of my life.'

'Dear me,' answered the lady, eyeing him uneasily, 'a morbid drunkard, are you? Well, as I am half perished with cold, suppose you take me to Kostopchin; you will be conferring a favour on me, and will get back all the sooner to your favourite brandy.'

She placed her hand upon Paul's arm as she spoke, and mechanically he led the way to the great solitary white house. The few servants betrayed no astonishment at the appearance of the lady, for some of the serfs on their way back to the village had spread the report of the sudden appearance of the mysterious stranger; besides, they were not accustomed to question the acts of their somewhat arbitrary master.

Alexis and Katrina had gone to bed, and Paul and his guest sat down to a hastily improvised meal.

'I am no great eater,' remarked the lady, as she played with the food before her; and Paul noticed with surprise that scarcely a morsel passed her lips, though she more than once filled and emptied a goblet of the champagne which had been opened in honour of her arrival.

'So it seems,' remarked he; 'and I do not wonder, for the food in this benighted hole is not what either you or I have been accustomed to.'

'Oh, it does well enough,' returned the lady, carelessly. 'And now, if you have such a thing as a woman in the establishment, you can let her show me to my room, for I am nearly dead for want of sleep.'

Paul struck a hand-bell that stood on the table beside him, and the stranger rose from her seat, and with a brief 'Good night', was moving towards the door, when the old man Michal suddenly made his appearance on the threshold. The aged intendant started backwards as though to avoid a heavy blow, and his fingers at once sought for the crucifix which he wore suspended round his neck, and on whose protection he relied to shield him from the powers of darkness.

'Blessed Virgin!' he exclaimed. 'Holy Saint Radislas protect me, where have I seen her before?'

The lady took no notice of the old man's evident terror, but passed away down the echoing corridor.

The old man now timidly approached his master, who, after swallowing a glass of brandy, had drawn his chair up to the stove, and was gazing moodily at its polished surface.

'My lord,' said Michal, venturing to touch his master's shoulder, 'is that the lady that you found in the forest?'

'Yes,' returned Paul, a smile breaking out over his face; 'she is very beautiful, is she not?'

'Beautiful!' repeated Michal, crossing himself, 'she may have beauty, but it is that of a demon. Where have I seen her before? – Where have I seen those shining teeth and those cold eyes? She is not like anyone here, and I have never been ten versts from Kostopchin in my life. I am utterly bewildered. Ah, I have it, the dying herdsman – save the mark! Gospodin, have a care. I tell you that the strange lady is the image of the white wolf.'

'You old fool,' returned his master, savagely, 'let me ever hear you repeat such nonsense again, and I will have you skinned alive. The lady is high-born, and of good family; beware how you insult her. Nay, I give you further commands: see that during her sojourn here she is treated with the utmost respect. And communicate this to all the servants. Mind, no more tales about the vision that your addled brain conjured up of wolves in the marsh, and above all do not let me hear that you have been alarming little Katrina with your senseless babble.'

The old man bowed humbly, and, after a short pause, remarked: 'The lad that was injured at the hunt today is dead, my lord.'

'Oh, dead is he, poor wretch!' returned Paul, to whom the death of a serf lad was not a matter of overweening importance. 'But look here, Michal, remember that if any inquiries are made about the lady, that no-one knows anything about her; that, in fact, no-one has seen her at all.'

'Your lordship shall be obeyed,' answered the old man; and then, seeing that his master had relapsed into his former moody reverie, he left the room, crossing himself at every step he took.

Late into the night Paul sat up thinking over the occurrences of the day. He had told Michal that his guest was of noble family, but in reality he knew nothing more of her than she had condescended to tell him.'

'Why, I don't even know her name,' muttered he; 'and yet somehow or other it seems as if a new feature of my life was opening before me. However, I have made one step in advance by getting her here, and if she talks about leaving, why, all that I have to do is threaten her with the police.'

After his usual custom he smoked cigarette after cigarette, and poured out copious tumblers of brandy. The attendant serf replenished the stove from a small den which opened into the corridor, and after a time Paul slumbered heavily in his armchair. He was aroused by a light touch upon the shoulder, and, starting up, saw the stranger of the forest standing by his side.

'This is indeed kind of you,' said she, with her usual mocking smile. 'You felt that I should be strange here, and you got up early to see to the horses, or can it really be, those ends of cigarettes, that empty bottle of brandy? Paul Sergevitch, you have not been to bed at all.'

Paul muttered a few indistinct words in reply, and then, ringing the bell furiously, ordered the servant to clear away the débris of last night's orgy, and lay the table for breakfast; then, with a hasty apology, he left the room to make a fresh toilet, and in about half an hour returned with his appearance sensibly improved by his ablutions and change of dress.

'I dare say,' remarked the lady, as they were seated at the morning meal, for which she manifested the same indifference that she had for the dinner of the previous evening, 'that you would like to know my name and who I am. Well, I don't mind telling you my name. It is Ravina, but as to my family and who I am, it will perhaps be best for you to remain in ignorance. A matter of policy, my dear Paul Sergevitch, a mere matter of policy, you see. I leave you to judge from my manners and appearance whether I am of sufficiently good form to be invited to the honour of your table – '

'None more worthy,' broke in Paul, whose bemuddled brain was fast succumbing to the charms of his guest; 'and surely that is a question upon which I may be deemed a competent judge.'

'I do not know about that,' returned Ravina, 'for from all accounts the company that you used to keep was not of the most select character.'

'No, but hear me,' began Paul, seizing her hand and endeavouring to carry it to his lips. But as he did so an unpleasant chill passed over him, for those slender fingers were icy cold.

'Do not be foolish,' said Ravina, drawing away her hand, after she had permitted it to rest for an instant in Paul's grasp, 'do you not hear someone coming?'

As she spoke the sound of tiny pattering feet was heard in the corridor, then the door was flung violently open, and with a shrill cry of delight, Katrina rushed into the room, followed more slowly by her brother Alexis.

'And are these your children?' asked Ravina, as Paul took up the little girl and placed her fondly upon his knee, whilst the boy stood a few paces from the door gazing with eyes of wonder upon the strange woman, for whose appearance he was utterly unable to account. 'Come here, my little man,' continued she; 'I suppose you are the heir of Kostopchin, though you do not resemble your father much.'

'He takes after his mother, I think,' returned Paul carelessly; 'and how has my darling Katrina been?' he added, addressing his daughter.

'Quite well, papa dear,' answered the child; 'but where is the fine white wolf skin that you promised me?'

'Your father did not find her,' answered Ravina, with a little laugh; 'the white wolf was not so easy to catch as he fancied.'

Alexis had moved a few steps nearer to the lady, and was listening with grave attention to every word she uttered.

'Are white wolves so difficult to kill, then?' asked he.

'It seems so, my little man,' returned the lady, 'since your father and all the serfs of Kostopchin were unable to do so.'

'I have got a pistol, that good old Michal has taught me to fire, and I am sure I could kill her if ever I got sight of her,' observed Alexis, boldly.

'There is a brave boy,' returned Ravina, with one of her shrill laughs; 'and now, won't you come and sit on my knee, for I am very fond of little boys?'

'No, I don't like you,' answered Alexis, after a moment's consideration, 'for Michal says – '

'Go to your room, you insolent young brat,' broke in the father, in a voice of thunder. 'You spend so much of your time with Michal and the serfs that you have learned all their boorish habits.'

Two tiny tears rolled down the boy's cheeks as in obedience to his father's orders he turned about and quitted the room, whilst Ravina darted a strange look of dislike after him. As soon, however, as the door had closed, the fair woman addressed Katrina.

'Well, perhaps you will not be so unkind to me as your brother,' said she. 'Come to me,' and as she spoke she held out her arms.

The little girl came to her without hesitation, and began to smooth the silken tresses which were coiled and wreathed around Ravina's head.

'Pretty, pretty,' she murmured, 'beautiful lady.'

'You see, Paul Sergevitch, that your little daughter has taken to me at once,' remarked Ravina.

'She takes after her father, who was always noted for his good taste,' returned Paul, with a bow; 'but take care, madam, or the little puss will have your necklace off.'

The child had indeed succeeded in unclasping the glittering ornament, and was now inspecting it in high glee.

'That is a curious ornament,' said Paul, stepping up to the child and taking the circlet from her hand.

It was indeed a quaintly fashioned ornament, consisting as it did of a number of what were apparently curved pieces of sharp-pointed horn set in gold, and depending from a snake of the same precious metal.

'Why, these are claws,' continued he, as he looked at them more carefully.

'Yes, wolves' claws,' answered Ravina, taking the necklet from the child and reclasping it round her neck. 'It is a family relic which I have always worn.'

71

Katrina at first seemed inclined to cry at her new plaything being taken from her, but by caresses and endearments Ravina soon contrived to lull her once more into a good temper.

'My daughter has certainly taken to you in a most wonderful manner,' remarked Paul, with a pleased smile. 'You have quite obtained possession of her heart.'

'Not yet, whatever I may do later on,' answered the woman, with her strange cold smile, as she pressed the child closer towards her and shot a glance at Paul which made him quiver with an emotion that he had never felt before. Presently, however, the child grew tired of her new acquaintance, and sliding down from her knee, crept from the room in search of her brother Alexis.

Paul and Ravina remained silent for a few instants, and then the woman broke the silence.

'All that remains for me now, Paul Sergevitch, is to trespass on your hospitality, and to ask you to lend me some disguise, and assist me to gain the nearest post town, which, I think, is Vitroski.'

'And why should you wish to leave this place at all,' demanded Paul, a deep flush rising to his cheek. 'You are perfectly safe in my house, and if you attempt to pursue your journey there is every chance of your being recognised and captured.'

'Why do I wish to leave this house?' answered Ravina, rising to her feet and casting a look of surprise upon her interrogator. 'Can you ask me such a question? How is it possible for me to remain here?'

'It is perfectly impossible for you to leave; of that I am quite certain,' answered the man, doggedly. 'All I know is, that if you leave Kostopchin, you will inevitably fall into the hands of the police.'

'And Paul Sergevitch will tell them where they can find me?' questioned Ravina, with an ironical inflection in the tone of her voice.

'I never said so,' returned Paul.

'Perhaps not,' answered the woman, quickly, 'but I am not slow in reading thoughts; they are sometimes plainer to read than words. You are saying to yourself, 'Kostopchin is but a dull hole after all; chance has thrown into my hands a woman whose beauty pleases me; she is utterly friendless, and is in fear of the pursuit of the police; why should I not bend her to my will?' That is what you have been thinking, – is it not so, Paul Sergevitch?'

'I never thought, that is – ' stammered the man.

'No, you never thought that I could read you so plainly,' pursued the woman, pitilessly; 'but it is the truth that I have told you, and sooner than remain an inmate of your house, I would leave it, even if all the police of Russia stood ready to arrest me on its very threshold.'

'Stay, Ravina,' exclaimed Paul, as the woman made a step towards the door. 'I do not say whether your reading of my thoughts is right or wrong, but before you leave, listen to me. I do not speak to you in the usual strain of a pleading lover, – you, who know my past, would laugh at me should I do so; but I tell you plainly that from the first moment that I set eyes upon you, a strange new feeling has risen up in my heart, not the cold thing that society calls love, but a burning resistless flood which flows down like molten lava from the volcano's crater. Stay, Ravina, stay, I implore you, for if you go from here you will take my heart with you.'

'You may be speaking more truthfully than you think,' returned the fair woman, as, turning back, she came close up to Paul, and placing both her hands upon his shoulders, shot a glance of lurid fire from her eyes. 'Still, you have but given me a selfish reason for my staying, only your own self-gratification. Give me one that more nearly affects myself.'

Ravina's touch sent a tremor through Paul's whole frame which caused every nerve and sinew to vibrate. Gaze as boldly as he might into those steel-blue eyes, he could not sustain their intensity.

'Be my wife, Ravina,' faltered he. 'Be my wife. You are safe enough from all pursuit here, and if that does not suit you I can easily convert my estate into a large sum of money, and we can fly to other lands, where you can have nothing to fear from the Russian police.'

'And does Paul Sergevitch actually mean to offer his hand to a woman whose name he does not even know, and of whose feelings towards him he is entirely ignorant?' asked the woman, with her customary mocking laugh.

'What do I care for name or birth,' returned he, hotly, 'I have enough for both, and as for love, my passion would soon kindle some sparks of it in your breast, cold and frozen as it may now be.'

'Let me think a little,' said Ravina; and throwing herself into an armchair she buried her face in her hands and seemed plunged in deep reflection, whilst Paul paced impatiently up and down the room like a prisoner awaiting the verdict that would restore him to life or doom him to a shameful death.

At length Ravina removed her hands from her face and spoke.

'Listen,' said she. 'I have thought over your proposal seriously, and upon certain conditions, I will consent to become your wife.'

'They are granted in advance,' broke in Paul, eagerly.

'Make no bargains blindfold,' answered she, 'but listen. At the present moment I have no inclination for you, but on the other hand I feel no repugnance for you. I will remain here for a month, and during that time I shall remain in a suite of apartments which you will have prepared for me. Every evening I will visit you here, and upon your making yourself agreeable my ultimate decision will depend.'

'And suppose that decision should be an unfavourable one?' asked Paul.

'Then,' answered Ravina, with a ringing laugh, 'I shall, as you say, leave this house and take your heart with me.'

'These are hard conditions,' remarked Paul. 'Why not shorten the time of probation?'

'My conditions are unalterable,' answered Ravina, with a little stamp of the foot. 'Do you agree to them or not?'

'I have no alternative,' answered he, sullenly; 'but remember that I am to see you every evening.'

'For two hours,' said the woman, 'so you must try and make yourself as agreeable as you can in that time; and now, if you will give orders regarding my rooms, I will settle myself in them with as little delay as possible.'

Paul obeyed her, and in a couple of hours three handsome chambers were got ready for their fair occupant in a distant part of the great rambling house.

The awakening of the wolf

The days slipped slowly and wearily away, but Ravina showed no signs of relenting. Every evening, according to her bond, she spent two hours with Paul and made herself most agreeable, listening to his far-fetched compliments and asseverations of love and tenderness either with a cold smile or with one of her mocking laughs. She refused to allow Paul to visit her in her own apartments, and the only intruder she permitted there, save the servants, was little Katrina, who had taken a strange fancy to the fair woman. Alexis, on the contrary, avoided her as much as he possibly could, and the pair hardly ever met. Paul, to while away the time, wandered about the farm and the village, the inhabitants of which had recovered from their panic as the white wolf appeared to have entirely desisted from her murderous attacks upon belated peasants.

The shades of evening had closed in as Paul was one day returning from his customary round, rejoiced with the idea that the hour for

Ravina's visit was drawing near, when he was startled by a gentle touch upon the shoulder, and turning round, saw the old man Michal standing just behind him. The intendant's face was perfectly livid, his eyes gleamed with the lustre of terror, and his fingers kept convulsively clasping and unclasping.

'My lord,' exclaimed he, in faltering accents; 'oh, my lord, listen to me, for I have terrible news to narrate to you.'

'What is the matter?' asked Paul, more impressed than he would have liked to confess by the old man's evident terror.

'The wolf, the white wolf! I have seen it again,' whispered Michal.

'You are dreaming,' retorted his master, angrily. 'You have got the creature on the brain, and have mistaken a white calf or one of the dogs for it.'

'I am not mistaken,' answered the old man, firmly. 'And oh, my lord, do not go into the house, for she is there.'

'She – who – what do you mean?' cried Paul.

'The white wolf, my lord. I saw her go in. You know the strange lady's apartments are on the ground floor on the west side of the house. I saw the monster cantering across the lawn, and, as if it knew its way perfectly well, make for the centre window of the reception room; it yielded to a touch of the fore paw, and the beast sprang through. Oh, my lord, do not go in; I tell you that it will never harm the strange woman. Ah! let me – '

But Paul cast off the detaining arm with a force that made the old man reel and fall, and then, catching up an axe, dashed into the house, calling upon the servants to follow him to the strange lady's rooms. He tried the handle, but the door was securely fastened, and then, in all the frenzy of terror, he attacked the panels with heavy blows of his axe. For a few seconds no sound was heard save the ring of metal and the shivering of panels, but then the clear tones of Ravina were heard asking the reason for this outrageous disturbance.

'The wolf, the white wolf,' shouted half a dozen voices.

'Stand back and I will open the door,' answered the fair woman. 'You must be mad, for there is no wolf here.'

The door flew open and the crowd rushed tumultuously in; every nook and corner were searched, but no signs of the intruder could be discovered, and with many shamefaced glances Paul and his servants were about to return, when the voice of Ravina arrested their steps.'

'Paul Sergevitch,' sad she, coldly, 'explain the meaning of this daring intrusion on my privacy.'

She looked very beautiful as she stood before them, her right arm extended and her bosom heaving violently, but this was doubtless caused by her anger at the unlooked-for invasion.

Paul briefly repeated what he had heard from the old serf, and Ravina's scorn was intense.

'And so,' cried she, fiercely, 'it is to the crotchets of this old dotard that I am indebted for this. Paul, if you ever hope to succeed in winning me, forbid that man ever to enter the house again.'

Paul would have sacrificed all his serfs for a whim of the haughty beauty, and Michal was deprived of the office of intendant and exiled to a cabin in the village, with orders never to show his face again near the house. The separation from the children almost broke the old man's heart, but he ventured on no remonstrance and meekly obeyed the mandate which drove him away from all he loved and cherished.

Meanwhile, curious rumours began to be circulated regarding the strange proceedings of the lady who occupied the suite of apartments which had formerly belonged to the wife of the owner of Kostopchin. The servants declared that the food sent up, though hacked about and cut up, was never tasted, but that the raw meat in the larder was frequently missing. Strange sounds were often heard to issue from the rooms as the panic-stricken serfs hurried past the corridor upon which the doors opened, and dwellers in the house were frequently disturbed by the howlings of wolves, the footprints of which were distinctly visible the next morning, and, curiously enough, invariably in the gardens facing the west side of the house in which the lady dwelt. Little Alexis, who found no encouragement to sit with his father, was naturally thrown a great deal amongst the serfs, and heard the subject discussed with many exaggerations. Weird old tales of folklore were often narrated as the servants discussed their evening meal, and the boy's hair would bristle as he listened to the wild and fanciful narratives of wolves, witches, and white ladies with which the superstitious serfs filled his ears. One of his most treasured possessions was an old brass-mounted cavalry pistol, a present from Michal; this he had learned to load, and by using both hands to the cumbrous weapon could contrive to fire it off, as many an ill-starred sparrow could attest. With his mind constantly dwelling upon the terrible tales he had so greedily listened to, this pistol became his daily companion, whether he was wandering about the long echoing corridors of the house or wandering through the neglected shrubberies of the garden.

For a fortnight matters went on in this manner, Paul becoming more and more infatuated by the charms of his strange guest, and she every now and then letting drop occasional crumbs of hope which led the unhappy man further and further upon the dangerous course that he was pursuing. A mad, soul-absorbing passion for the fair woman and the deep draughts of brandy with which he consoled himself during her hours of absence were telling upon the brain of the master of Kostopchin, and except during the brief space of Ravina's visit, he would relapse into moods of silent sullenness from which he would occasionally break out into furious bursts of passion for no assignable cause. A shadow seemed to be closing over the house of Kostopchin; it became the abode of grim whispers and undeveloped fears; the men and maidservants went about their work glancing nervously over their shoulders, as though they were apprehensive that some hideous thing was following at their heels.

After three days of exile, poor old Michal could endure the state of suspense regarding the safety of Alexis and Katrina no longer; and, casting aside his superstitious fears, he took to wandering by night about the exterior of the great white house, and peering curiously into such windows as had been left unshuttered. At first he was in continual dread of meeting the terrible white wolf; but his love for the children and his confidence in the crucifix he wore prevailed, and he continued his nocturnal wanderings about Kostopchin and its environs. He kept near the western front of the house, urged on to do so from some vague feeling which he could in no wise account for. One evening as he was making his accustomed tour of inspection, the wail of a child struck upon his ear. He bent down his head and eagerly listened; again he heard the same faint sounds, and in them he fancied he recognised the accents of his dear little Katrina. Hurrying up to one of the ground-floor windows, from which a dim light streamed, he pressed his face against the pane, and looked steadily in. A horrible sight presented itself to his gaze. By the faint light of a shaded lamp, he saw Katrina stretched upon the ground; but her wailing had now ceased, for a shawl had been tied across her little mouth. Over her was bending a hideous shape, which seemed to be clothed in some white and shaggy covering. Katrina lay perfectly motionless, and the hands of the figure were engaged in hastily removing the garments from the child's breast. The task was soon effected; then there was a bright gleam of steel, and the head of the thing bent closely down to the child's bosom.

With a yell of apprehension, the old man dashed in the window frame, and, drawing the cross from his breast, sprang boldly into the room. The creature sprang to its feet, and the white fur cloak falling from its had and shoulders disclosed the pallid features of Ravina, a short, broad knife in her hand, and her lips discoloured with blood.

'Vile sorceress!' cried Michal, dashing forward and raising Katrina in his arms. 'What hellish work are you about?'

Ravina's eyes gleamed fiercely upon the old man, who had interfered between her and her prey. She raised her dagger, and was about to spring in upon him, when she caught sight of the cross in his extended hand. With a low cry, she dropped the knife, and, staggering back a few paces, wailed out: 'I could not help it; I liked the child well enough, but I was so hungry.'

Michal paid but little heed to her words, for he was busily engaged in examining the fainting child, whose head was resting helplessly on his shoulder. There was a wound over the left breast, from which the blood was flowing; but the injury appeared slight, and not likely to prove fatal. As soon as he had satisfied himself on this point, he turned to the woman, who was crouching before the cross as a wild beast shrinks before the whip of the tamer.

'I am going to remove the child,' said he, slowly. 'Dare you to mention a word of what I have done or whither she has gone, and I will arouse the village. Do you know what will happen then? Why, every peasant in the place will hurry here with a lighted brand in his hand to consume this accursed house and the unnatural dwellers in it. Keep silence, and I leave you to your unhallowed work. I will no longer seek to preserve Paul Sergevitch, who has given himself over to the powers of darkness by taking a demon to his bosom.'

Ravina listened to him as if she scarcely comprehended him; but, as the old man retreated to the window with his helpless burden, she followed him step by step; and as he turned to cast one last glance at the shattered window, he saw the woman's pale face and blood-stained lips glued against an unbroken pane, with a wild look of unsatiated appetite in her eyes.

Next morning the house of Kostopchin was filled with terror and surprise, for Katrina, the idol of her father's heart, had disappeared, and no signs of her could be discovered. Every effort was made, the woods and fields in the neighbourhood were thoroughly searched; but it was at last concluded that robbers had carried off the child for the sake of the ransom that they might be able to extract from the father. This seemed the more likely as one of the windows in the fair stranger's room bore marks of violence, and she declared that, being alarmed by the sound of crashing glass, she had risen and confronted a man who was endeavouring to enter her apartment, but who, on perceiving her, turned and fled away with the utmost precipitation.

Paul Sergevitch did not display as much anxiety as might have been expected from him, considering the devotion which he had ever evinced for the lost Katrina, for his whole soul was wrapped up in one mad, absorbing passion for the fair woman who had so strangely crossed his life. He certainly directed the search, and gave all the necessary orders; but he did so in a listless and half-hearted manner, and hastened back to Kostopchin as speedily as he could as though fearing to be absent for any length of time from the casket in which his new treasure was enshrined. Not so Alexis; he was almost frantic at the loss of his sister, and accompanied the searchers daily until his little legs grew weary, and he had to be carried on the shoulders of a sturdy moujik. His treasured brass-mounted pistol was now more than ever his constant companion; and when he met the fair woman who had cast a spell upon his father, his face would flush, and he would grind his teeth in impotent rage.

The day upon which all search had ceased, Ravina glided into the room where she knew that she would find Paul awaiting her. She was fully an hour before her usual time, and the lord of Kostopchin started to his feet in surprise.

'You are surprised to see me,' said she; 'but I have only come to pay you a visit for a few minutes. I am convinced that you love me, and could I but relieve a few of the objections that my heart continues to raise, I might be yours.'

'Tell me what these scruples are,' cried Paul, springing towards her, and seizing her hands in his; 'and be sure that I will find means to overcome them.'

Even in the midst of all the glow and fervour of anticipated triumph, he could not avoid noticing how icily cold were the fingers that rested in his palm, and how utterly passionless was the pressure with which she slightly returned his enraptured clasp.

'Listen,' said she, as she withdrew her hand; 'I will take two more hours for consideration. By that time the whole of the house of Kostopchin will be cradled in slumber; then meet me at the old sundial near the yew tree at the bottom of the garden, and I will give you my reply. Nay, not a word,' she added, as he seemed about to remonstrate, 'for I tell you that I think it will be a favourable one.'

'But why not come back here?' urged he; 'there is a hard frost tonight, and – '

'Are you so cold a lover,' broke in Ravina, with her accustomed laugh, 'to dread the changes of the weather? But not another word; I have spoken.'

She glided from the room, but uttered a low cry of rage. She had almost fallen over Alexis in the corridor.

'Why is that brat not in his bed? ' cried she, angrily; 'he gave me quite a turn.'

'Go to your room, boy,' exclaimed his father, harshly; and with a malignant glance at his enemy, the child slunk away.

Paul Sergevitch paced up and down the room for the two hours that he had to pass before the hour of meeting. His heart was very heavy, and a vague feeling of disquietude began to creep over him. Twenty times he made up his mind not to keep his appointment, and as often the fascination of the fair woman compelled him to rescind his resolution. He remember that he had from childhood disliked that spot by the yew tree, and had always looked upon it as a dreary, uncanny place; and he even now disliked the idea of finding himself here after dark, even with such fair companionship as he had been promised. Counting the minutes, he paced backwards and forwards, as though moved by some concealed machinery. Now and again he glanced at the clock, and at last its deep metallic sound, as it struck the quarter, warned him that he had but little time to lose, if he intended to keep his appointment. Throwing on a heavily furred coat and pulling a travelling cap down over his ears, he opened a side door and sallied out into the grounds. The moon was at its full, and shone coldly down upon the leafless trees, which looked white and ghostlike in its beams. The paths and unkept lawns were now covered with hoar frost, and a keen wind every now and then swept by, which, in spite of his wraps, chilled Paul's blood in his veins. The dark shape of the yew tree soon rose up before him, and in another moment he stood beside its dusky boughs. The old grey sundial stood only a few paces off, and by its side was standing a slender figure, wrapped in a white, fleecy-looking cloak. It was perfectly motionless, and again a terror of undefined dread passed through every nerve and muscle of Paul Sergevitch's body.

'Ravina!' said he, in faltering accents. 'Ravina!'

'Did you take me for a ghost?' answered the fair woman, with her shrill laugh; 'no, no, I have not come to that yet. Well, Paul Serge-vitch, I have come to give you my answer; are you anxious about it?'

'How can you ask me such a question?' returned he; 'do you not know that my whole soul has been aglow with anticipations of what your reply might be? Do not keep me any longer in suspense. Is it yes, or no?'

'Paul Sergevitch,' answered the young woman, coming up to him and laying her hands upon his shoulders, and fixing her eyes upon his with that strange weird expression before which he always quailed; 'do you really love me, Paul Sergevitch?' asked she.

'Love you!' repeated the lord of Kostopchin; 'have I not told you a thousand times how much my whole soul flows out towards you, how I only live and breathe in your presence, and how death at your feet would be more welcome than life without you?'

'People often talk of death, and yet little know how near it is to them,' answered the fair lady, a grim smile appearing upon her face; 'but say, do you give me your whole heart?'

'All I have is yours, Ravina,' returned Paul, 'name, wealth, and the devoted love of a lifetime.'

'But your heart,' persisted she; 'it is your heart that I want; tell me, Paul, that it is mine and mine only.'

'Yes, my heart is yours, dearest Ravina,' answered Paul, endeavouring to embrace the fair form in his impassioned grasp; but she glided from him, and then with a quick bound sprang upon him and glared in his face with a look that was absolutely appalling. Her eyes gleamed with a lurid fire, her lips were drawn back, showing her sharp, white teeth, whilst her breath came in sharp, quick gasps.

'I am hungry,' she murmured, 'oh, so hungry; but now, Paul Sergevitch, your heart is mine.'

Her movement was so sudden and unexpected that he stumbled and fell heavily to the ground, the fair woman clinging to him and falling upon his breast. It was then that the full horror of his position came upon Paul Sergevitch, and he saw his fate clearly before him; but a terrible numbness prevented him from using his hands to free himself from the hideous embrace which was paralysing all his muscles. The face that was glaring into his seemed to be undergoing some fearful change, and the features to be losing their semblance of humanity. With a sudden, quick movement, she tore open his garments, and in another moment she had perforated his left breast with a ghastly wound, and, plunging in her delicate hands, tore out his heart and bit at it ravenously. Intent upon her hideous banquet she heeded not the convulsive struggles which agitated the dying form of the lord of Kostopchin. She was too much occupied to notice a diminutive form approaching, sheltering itself behind every tree and bush until it had arrived within ten paces of the scene of the terrible tragedy. Then the moonbeams glistened upon the long shining barrel of a pistol, which a boy was levelling with both hands at the murderess. Then quick and sharp rang out the report, and with a wild shriek, in which there was something beastlike, Ravina leaped from the body of the dead man and staggered away to a thick clump of bushes some ten paces distant. The boy Alexis had heard the appointment that had been made, and dogged his father's footsteps to the trysting place. After firing the fatal shot his courage deserted him, and he fled backwards to the house, uttering loud shrieks for help. The startled servants were soon in the presence of their slaughtered master, but aid was of no avail, for the lord of Kostopchin had passed away. With fear and trembling the superstitious peasants searched the clump of bushes, and started back in horror as they perceived a huge white wolf, lying stark and dead, with a half-devoured human heart clasped between its forepaws.

* * *

No signs of the fair lady who had occupied the apartments in the western side of the house were ever again seen. She had passed away from Kostopchin like an ugly dream, and as the moujiks of the village sat around their stoves at night they whispered strange stories regarding the fair woman of the forest and the white wolf of Kostopchin. By order of the Tsar a surtee was placed in charge of the estate of Kostopchin, and Alexis was ordered to be sent to a military school until he should be old enough to join the army. The meeting between the boy and his sister, whom the faithful Michal, when all danger was at an end, had produced from his hiding place, was most affecting; but it was not until Katrina had been for some time resident at the house of a distant relative at Vitepak, that she ceased to wake at night and cry out in terror as she again dreamed that she was in the clutches of the white wolf.

The Thing in the Forest

BERNARD CAPES

Into the snow-locked forests of Upper Hungary steal wolves in winter; but there is a footfall worse than theirs to knock upon the heart of the lonely traveller.

One December evening Elspet, the young, newly wedded wife of the woodman Stefan, came hurrying over the lower slopes of the White Mountains from the town where she had been all day marketing. She carried a basket with provisions on her arm; her plump cheeks were like a couple of cold apples; her breath spoke short, but more from nervousness than exhaustion. It was nearing dusk, and she was glad to see the little lonely church in the hollow below, the hub, as it were, of many radiating paths through· the trees, one of which was the road to her own warm cottage yet a half-mile away.

She paused a moment at the foot of the slope, undecided about entering the little chill, silent building 'and making her plea for protection to the great battered stone image of Our Lady of Succour which stood within by the confessional box; but the stillness and the growing darkness decided her, and she went on. A spark of fire glowing through the presbytery window seemed to repel rather than attract her, and she was glad when the convolutions of the path hid it from her sight. Being new to the district, she had seen very little of Father Ruhl as yet, and somehow the penetrating knowledge and burning eyes of the pastor made her feel uncomfortable.

The soft drift, the lane of tall, motionless pines, stretched on in a quiet like death. Somewhere the sun, like a dead fire, had fallen into opalescent embers faintly luminous: they were enough only to touch the shadows with a ghastlier pallor. It was so still that the light crunch in the snow of the girl's own footfalls trod on her heart like a desecration.

Suddenly there was something near her that had not been before. It had come like a shadow, without more sound or warning. It was here – there – behind her. She turned, in mortal panic, and saw a wolf. With a strangled cry and trembling limbs she strove to hurry on her way; and always she knew, though there was no whisper of pursuit, that the gliding shadow followed in her wake. Desperate in her terror, she stopped once more and faced it.

A wolf! – Was it a wolf? O who could doubt it! Yet the wild expression in those famished eyes, so lost, so pitiful, so mingled of insatiable hunger and human need! Condemned, for its unspeakable sins, to take this form with sunset, and so howl and snuffle about the doors of men until the blessed day released it. A werewolf – not a wolf.

That terrific realisation of the truth smote the girl as with a knife out of darkness: for an instant she came near fainting. And then a low moan broke into her heart and flooded it with pity. So lost, so infinitely hopeless. And so pitiful – yes, in spite of all, so pitiful. It had sinned, beyond any sinning that her innocence knew or her experience could gauge; but she was a woman, very blest, very happy, in her store of comforts and her surety of love. She knew that it was forbidden to succour these damned and nameless outcasts, to help or sympathise with them in any way. But there was good store of meat in her basket, and who need ever know or tell? With shaking hands she found and threw a sop to the desolate brute – then, turning, sped upon her way.

But at home her secret sin stood up before her, and, interposing between her husband and herself, threw its shadow upon both their faces. What had she dared – what done? By her own act forfeited her birthright of innocence; by her own act placed herself in the power of the evil to which she had ministered. All that night she lay in shame and horror, and all the next day, until Stefan had come about his dinner and gone again, she moved in a dumb agony. Then, driven unendurably by the memory of his troubled, bewildered face, as twilight threatened she put on her cloak and went down to the little church in the hollow to confess her sin.

'Mother, forgive, and save me,' she whispered, as she passed the statue.

After ringing the bell for the confessor, she had not knelt long at the confessional box in the dim chapel, cold and empty as a waiting vault, when the chancel rail clicked, and the footsteps of Father Ruhl were heard rustling over the stones. He came, he took his seat behind the grating; and, with many sighs and falterings, Elspet avowed her guilt. And as, with bowed head, she ended, a strange sound answered her – it was like a little laugh, and yet not so much like a laugh as a snarl. With a shock as of death she raised her face. It was Father Ruhl who sat there – and yet it was not Father Ruhl. In that time of twilight his face was already changing, narrowing, becoming wolfish – the eyes rounded and the jaw slavered. She gasped, and shrunk back; and at that, barking and snapping at the grating, with a wicked look he dropped – and she heard him coming. Sheer horror lent her wings. With a scream she sprang to her feet and fled. Her cloak caught in something – there was a wrench and crash and, like a flood, oblivion overswept her.

It was the old deaf and near senile sacristan who found them lying there, the woman unhurt but insensible, the priest crushed out of life by the fall of the ancient statue, long tottering to its collapse. She recovered, for her part: for his, no-one knows where he lies buried. But there were dark stories of a baying pack that night, and of an empty, bloodstained pavement when they came to seek for the body.

Among the Wolves

VASILE VOICULESCU

'We were talking about big game and major hunts, gradually abandoned here though our mountains still teem with huge bears, proud
stags, ominous black goats and dangerous boars; the lynx and the
marten, however, fewer in number.

'The auroch alone is missing in the old hunting fauna of this
country. It's a pity we didn't breed them again, as other countries
did' – the host added.

'I have long been saying so,' another man put in. 'This is a spot
where impassioned hunters could easily meet the emotions and
adventures of big game hunting, no need to go tearing to Africa
or India.'

The talk kept coming back to the decadence of this vital and
ancestral activity: hunting. Man had brought it from the depths
of the stone age when he had had to fight alone an unequal battle
with the cave bear and the native lion. Most of all with the elk,
the bold stag of primitive eras, more dangerous than all the beasts
together.

Someone asked a question about the elk. The host instantly
produced sketch-books with copies from drawings found in caves
presenting wonderful primitive hunting scenes. He also brought
books about the role and importance of hunting in the prehistoric
period. Leaning over them we began to realise that the struggle with
wild creatures far stronger than ourselves, forced us into becoming
human beings in order to get the better of them.

The host explained that for food man could find plenty of booty
weaker than he was, as well as all the fruits of the earth. But against
the lion invading his cavern; against the bear with whom he was
competing for shelter, or against the mammoth who simply crushed
him, hunting was bound to become the supreme art, both knowledge
and witchcraft, technique and culture, sacrifice and tense energy,
using puppets and magic ritual as displayed on the walls of altars,

such as they appear in all the paintings of prehistoric caves. As still practised by present day savages.

Here and there,' he continued, 'far-sounding echoes are still to be heard in the magic practices and superstitions of rural hunters: the charmed bullet, the magic salves, talismans, auspicious or ill-fated days, and other ceremonials of hunting going as far as purification. A true huntsman does not smoke tobacco and abstains from drinking spirits, at least while hunting.

'But no-one troubles to store and treasure the dust of this shattered culture, formerly the embodiment, the essence of human ideal,' he concluded with a sigh.

Deeply moved, our thoughts were turning back along the paths cut by palaeolithic men, to the caverns strewn with bones of bears and lions pacified and buried with incantations and charms by the clan's wise men.

After a brief silence, a lawyer put the book down and asked permission to tell a personal experience that he was just beginning to understand in all its implications.

'I was justice of the peace in a rural district,' he began, 'all hilly, wooded country at the foot of the mountains. Angry rivers had formerly torn the earth apart so that huge precipices with horizontal layers of purple clay interspersed with white grit-stone gave a shocking impression of primeval archaism. Nowhere have I seen the sky rent by such deep, mysterious sunsets, shedding over regions petrified in immemorial time, the yellow anaemic blood of èras long gone by. I wouldn't be surprised to hear that the black hollows yawning in the steep sides of the precipice were openings of caverns full of bones of the past such as the ones in the books we've just been looking at. The district was still rich in game, mostly wolves and foxes, even martens and lynxes, but shooting did not interest me. In those days, I was merely thinking of my position, of my promotion, and a quick release from that place. However, I had begun collecting rudiments of common law and samples of local customs in view of a study meant to keep me busy.

The low bowing and the fear in people's looks were not the only surprise. Such kow-towing met all of us who belonged to the administration. And reasonably too. I dealt out penalties, didn't I? There was something more, however, that impressed me: a kind of reverence, a veneration of a different kind greeted me, not granted to my colleagues the medical man and the sub-prefect. I soon understood. I was a wise man, a magus. The judge was considered over and above the others, invested with spiritual powers. I did not beat people like the gendarme or the county chief. Nor did I grab sick children out of their mothers' arms, like the doctor, to send them to hospital. As a judge a single written line of mine could tie or untie whatever the others devised: fines, infringement of the law, law-suits. My mere signature was enough to rid the offender of all the sins that had brought him before me. Nor could the clergyman do this, who, as a matter of fact, was wrangling with and suing the villagers.

One day I acquitted a peasant charged with poaching in forbidden season and shooting forbidden game. To cap it all: a doe. The gendarme had caught him in the act of flaying it.

The man protested that he hadn't shot it nor trapped it, but redeemed it from the fangs of wolves who had been driving it hard. Actually, upon enquiry, no bullet marks had been found, just the traces of fangs deep sunk into the prey's neck torn and mangled by beasts. The people of the village, however, appeared discontented with my verdict. Some with whom I was on friendly terms ventured to say so. The man had taken me in. He had been poaching and should have been punished. The fact that bullet marks had not been found was no proof at all.

'What are you talking about?' I said. 'You've all seen the doe's neck mangled by wolves' fangs.'

'Yes, but the wolves were working for him. He set them on.'

'Set them on, did you say?' I asked in wonder. 'You won't tell me that wolves are as good as hounds in these parts.'

'It's just as you say,' they confirmed. 'The beasts wait upon him as if hired. They chase and kill the game by order. Nay, place it at his feet. How else could he get it out of the pack's jaws, if not by agreement? They would tear him to tatters, too.'

Quite true. At the hearing I never thought of asking the accused how he had managed to get the prey from the wolves.

On this occasion I learnt that my man was known as a wolf-tamer, subjecting them by means of charms and magic, and using them like a master.

They called him the Wolfer and he was considered ta be one of the freaks of nature. I became interested and went to see him. He could have been of help in my research into peasant tradition, as well as an intersting human type.

He was living like an outcast away from the village, in the wilderness, in a kind of half-hovel, half-cavern, dug into the clay of a desolate hillside. He had no wife, no child, nothing whatever. He was alone like a hermit. People said he couldn't bear any tame animal usually found in human households to live by his side. Cattle would run away frightened at the sight of him and dogs would scuttle away howling.

In fact no live creature came to meet me as I entered his yard. Poverty, I said to myself, that's all. Just a few hens bathing in the dust. I called. He took his time in coming. He was glad to see me. A vigorous old man, lean, tall and bony, gloomy yet eyes sharp and singeing, thick hair falling upon his brow, broad hands with fingers spread out like paws. The long olive-coloured face was almost glabrous, framed by a collar of thin prickly beard under the jaws. There was something secret, sad, yet vehement in this face.

So I understood why he was the terror and the curse of the village, for they actually hated and hooted him. He looked abnormal, the Lombroso criminal type. People said that a fierce reeking smell came out of his body and that none could bear either his smell or his gaze. I tried to sift the truth from the blame that people were piling upon him; they accused him of much evil and foul deeds, more especially that he was purposefully sending the wolves to work havoc among the cattle of the farmers. Nay, he sometimes would himself turn into a wolf, attacking the men to tear them to pieces.

The Wolfer received me awkwardly but decently, no kow-towing, with a dignity and self-control that impressed me. I stepped up to him. You could actually feel a strong smell. I wonder if any of you ever skinned a serpent. Well now, he had a sharp smack, as of arsenic. But I think it came from a fur jacket that he was wearing, as well as from the fur waistband wrapped tight against his slim waist, as slim as a young man's.

He asked me inside his den. There was a fire burning in the grate and a pot of weeds was boiling. The bench too was covered with hides of beasts. Hides everywhere: of bears, of wolves, of does.

I asked why he had shot them. He said they were old ones, mostly inherited from his father and grandfather. Some, since he had formerly been carrying a gun like every huntsman, long ago. But now, in his old age, unable to take aim, he had given up shooting. He would lay snares and set traps, occasionally catching a fox grown vicious for fowls; or still more seldom would he recapture a prey from the wolves, by clubbing at them, as it happened with the doe for which he had been driven to law by his enemies. But as he grew older it was ever more difficult. His strength on the wane, he was waiting for the wild beasts to tear him to pieces some day.

I took the opportunity of his talking about wild beasts, openly confessing my interest in his relations with wild things, wolves in particular. That's what I had come for. The man considered me without blinking and was silent. I pleaded to have come out of real friendly feeling for him, in no way to spy or sound him. That I too was experimenting a kind of magic or incantation to call up the spirits of the dead – I was actually practising spiritualism – and I asked him to impart the secret of his knowledge and strength. He pleaded that the world's slander held no truth, that he didn't know and couldn't do anything beyond what other men could do. But that he had the knack of talking to wolves in their own language and making himself understood.

'You know the speech of the wolves, do you?'

'Yes sir. I learnt it as a small child.'

'How did you and who from?'

'From grandfather and from father, they both knew.'

'Did they, really?'

'They did. Grandfather and father were foresters, always had been. They lived at the heart of the forest and reared wolves that they caught when cubs. I was born and bred among wolf whelps, eating side by side with them, playing and wrestling till my folks came late at night, from the wilderness. Here, you can still see the marks of their fangs and claws.'

He bared his arms, hairy stumps, all sinews, knots and lumps.

'What about your mother?' I asked.

'I had no mother,' was the brief answer.

'And your wife?'

'My wife is a bushy hollow in the woods.'

I realised that along this line everything was sore to the touch. I changed the subject.

'What did your people do with the wolves?'

'They kept them just for company,' the man said with a bitter smile.

'Just that much?'

'Nay they would also keep away men and beasts from the den.'

I went on considering him inquiringly.

'Occasionally they would help them catch,' the man completed his answer to my enquiry.

'But,' he added, 'as soon as they grew up and felt the urge of love, they would break the chains and run back into the forest, forgetful of human friendliness and a settled life.'

'So they actually were like dogs to you.'

'Wild things, nevertheless, sir; no way of thoroughly taming them. Father's hands and legs were all marks and sores, bitten in by them. They had to be crammed with meat to allow you anywhere near them, to fondle them and get the prey out of their jaws.'

Confession after confession. The Wolfer went as far as to promise to take me one suitable night to show me his skill with the wolves.

He chose the night before St Andrew's Day when wolves were to get their yearly portion of booty. They were each granted one special man, woman or child that they were allowed to eat. No more! There was no reckoning for cattle and other booty. They could have as many as they liked. As regards man alone the wolf had to be content with his appointed portion. It was a kind of right – I set this down for my study – a fragment of the old code of laws governing primitive hunting. I sounded him concerning other superstitions and heresies. He answered truthfully and intelligently.

I was moved by the haunted and abused man standing before me; it was not pity for the loneliness he had been driven into by an adverse society, but rather an active interest for his toughness in the struggle for life, for his firmness in opposing a hostile world of people who were actual brutes to him.

As I was leaving he wished to present me with a fur cap full of freshly laid eggs. I refused. He quickly rummaged in a trunk and produced a few marten hides, sheer beauties. I did not take them. He realised that I was not the kind to be after presents, so he did not insist.

It was settled that on the eve of St Andrew's Day I should call on him. I did not want the village to get wind of what I was doing and interfere in my affairs. That was about three weeks ahead.

I can't say I had forgotten about our meeting. But my interest had subsided to such an extent that I was loath to face the cold and go out. I had other worries now. I was actually waiting for urgent summons from Bucharest pending my transfer to the law courts. A possible trip to Bucharest in order to hasten my promotion, was a real bother since there was no-one to leave in charge for a couple of days.

So the day promised to the Wolfer had quite slipped out of my mind.

One night I was suddenly wakened by the shrieking and hooting in the village and all the farm hands bustling about. Two wolves had boldly entered the country court residence where I was staying and tried to steal the usher's pig. That made me keep my word, so that the following night, my gun across my shoulder, I made for the Wolfer's den.

'I got your message,' I shouted joking. 'You were right to send it, I had a mind to stop bothering you.'

'Why no, sir,' he said with glistening eyes, 'no bother at all. Please to come in till the dark dispels, for the moon shall soon rise.'

I walked in. In the gleam of a rushlight I then saw that which I hadn't noticed before: on the whitewashed walls, large and small figures of wolves, stags, foxes and wild boars, some drawn in charcoal, others in red clay, in various positions. Some were running, others were laid low, some in unlikely attitudes like standing up on their hind legs or up in widely-branching trees. In the midst of these images there was a huge man with a gigantic club, as if he were driving them on. His outline went beyond the wall, stretching out upon the low ceiling, like a protecting divinity.

There was a wonderful firmness and skill in the drawing, as if by some really gifted hand.

'Childish nonsense,' the man said, watching my amazement with displeasure. 'I'm in my second childhood, so that in the winter, to while away the time, I play as I used to in father's hut.'

Looking around I saw on the stove and in various corners other animal figures made of clay. These were coarser, such as those that are sold at fairs. Some were lame, with one leg missing, some had holes in the ribs, some were pierced with pikes.

I tried to examine them more closely. But the Wolfer stopped me.

'Ready, your Honour,' he solemnly announced, rising in front of me and obscuring the view. 'The moon's out and we'd better be going, it's a good bit to walk.'

I had to leave alone the clay idols and follow him. He had only taken an enormous club. He wore a long mantle of wild animal hides, wolves' I think, which, reeked with that insufferable sharp smell now all over the man.

We walked some two hours, in a roundabout way, climbing up and down hills and hillocks, now barren, now thick with tangled woods till we reached a hill top dominating the valleys. Now that I think it over, I don't believe we got very far, but the man took me round about to conceal his tracks, as beasts do. Or maybe – But the place we stopped at was sunk in silence, solitude and frost, as on a lifeless planet. The stunning moonlight making everything look even more fantastic, was enveloping, isolating, secluding it even more from the rest of the world.

The Wolfer helped me climb a wide-branched oak tree where he had contrived a small bed out of a few armfuls of maize stalks, in between two strong branches. Then he, too, climbed higher *up to the top.*

Nothing budged in the freezing moonlight that glazed the whole visible world in its frost. My heart alone was nervously thumping.

Suddenly, from above, bitter weeping bubbled forth, a sorrowful yelping, rapidly changing into a monstrous, prolonged, modulated howl, gurgling and gushing. Had I not quickly grabbed at something and planted myself squarely in the tree's branches, I should have tumbled down. I looked up. Perching upon a branch that he clung to with both arms, the man rose above the crown of the tree. His face was bent upon a thing that he was holding in both hands out of which came that frightful wailing. He stopped a few minutes, the surrounding stillness seeming to prick its ears expectantly. Then the strange lullaby began again, a dramatic appeal, a kind of scream of the wilderness and a perplexity at the same time. Then the tragic chanting was quiet again, in expectation.

From afar a loud dirge-like call, as if from a wooden horn, sounded fiercely.

The man called again. From another corner of the world a still more horrible howl answered. Soon a dialogue or rather a polylogue grew ever stronger, a savage mimicking between the Wolfer and the Unseen whose sorrowful tones approached on padded feet, drawn by the ever more urging clamour of the Wizard.

Suddenly, with all my instincts awake, I felt a presence. I looked down. At the foot of the tree a wild beast was looking up, considering us. Swiftly another wolf slipped alongside, silently. The man went on calling long and mournfully to the four winds, wherefrom answers came ever more dismal, lamentations close or distant as if spinning round in a blizzard, hoarse chanting, cries, ho there! strangled in hungry gullets, like the shrieks of boundless desolation, of endless hopelessness.

The tree was soon surrounded by a pack of wolves, placed in a circle, sitting on their hind legs as if in conference. Necks tense, eyes shining, they were softly yelping between their teeth, with rumblings and flourishes, in different registers and tones, flat and sharp notes, in conversation with the man. He was now modulating his incantation in short syncopated rhythms as if in a predicament, from sepulchral grave sounds to the velvety voice of the flute, and the fearful shrillness of crime. Down below savage vocalising was alternating with thoughtful silence.

What was the man saying? Was he telling them a tale? Was he scolding them? Promising something? Sharing out the spoils, each one his lot? Because the wolves, gullets turned upwards, kept changing places, creeping upon their bellies, springing to their feet; then started wailing, chattering their teeth as if dancing to the master's tune. I couldn't tell how long this circus-like show lasted. I was more than dizzy and bewildered. I sat there hypnotised, stunned, my hands clinging fast to a branch, the gun useless on my knees. I didn't feel the cold but I must have been frozen to the bone, for I was rigid like an icicle. I then came to my senses. At a move the gun started slipping down. I tried to catch hold of it, but I toppled over with the pile of maize stalks on which I had turned to stone; rolling over several times, I was down at the root of the tree surrounded by wild beasts who all rose at the same moment, their hairs bristling.

Before any of them had broken the circle and jumped, the Wolfer had dropped from the top right into the midst of them – tempestuous, the club raised like a sceptre, with a fearful roar.

As I lay looking up at him, he looked enormous, his fluffy coat shaggy and the pointed cap obscuring the moon that formed a kind of halo round his head. Eyes agog glowed with a kind of flame, as well as his outstretched hands, particularly his fingers: a sort of phosphorescent essence as that of glow-worms. And the strong scent, the insufferable reeking that no-one could abide, now still sharper, exuded from his body with unbearable force.

The wolves were stunned; the man stuck his head again into a pot – I could now see clearly – and swiftly started producing ever shorter, more commanding sounds, like the panting, smothered gurgling of a savage gullet. Hearing this the wolves, their tails sagging, began to draw back, loosening the loop around us.

'Climb instantly up the tree,' the Wolfer ordered me in a low voice, half his muzzle out of the pot still astir with howling echoes.

I tried to stand up but could not. There was a sharp pain in my ankle.

'I can't,' said I moaning, 'I've broken my ankle.'

The man crouched down, with his back close to me. 'Cling to my back, quick.' – And he crouched into as low a heap as he could, that I might reach him and put my arms round his neck: I was then still slim and no weight.

The man rose, myself clinging to him, he shook himself to give me a good seat along his broad back and made his way with the burden on his back, never stopping those magic sounds and the many-voiced converse with the wild things no longer in a loop but now gathering into a pack again, the large beast heading it.

I contracted my knees and raised my feet that my toes should not trail on the ground, stumbling against stones or roots. So I clung to him deeply breathing in that magic scent that held the beasts in check, of which I now felt the full magic power. His hands went on sending forth the phosphorescent blaze, through the fingers mostly. I could see it before us when he reached out and rolled the club towards the wild things which drew back step by step, receding in front of him.

A few hesitations and the pack gave up. The magic poise required that there should be no blood. A single drop from man or beast would have broken the magic. Nothing could have stopped a catastrophe. But the Wolfer had won.

The howling, sounding ever more remote, smothered by moonlight and silence as by a shroud, gradually vanished beyond our horizon. What followed I don't know. I think I fainted with strain and pain, or possibly simply fell asleep. What I do know is that I woke up in my own bed at the justice's residence. It was broad daylight and the usher had brought me coffee in bed, as usual.

How the man had slunk in unseen and unheard bearing me on his back, remains a mystery. If it hadn't been for the pain in the ankle I should have been certain of having dreamt it all.

The medical man found that it was a mere sprained ankle. He wrapped it in a tight bandage and I could walk, my foot in a snowshoe, leaning on a stick. I couldn't keep to my bed. There had been a wire that very morning summoning me urgently to Bucharest for transfer. I packed my things and left like mad.

'What about the Wolfer?' the host asked.

'I can't tell you more. I left everything behind, never looking back, never giving it another thought. Once in Bucharest, entering a big career, I had to turn wizard myself, for a different kind of wild beasts, men with whom, as you know, I waged a hard battle.

'But your talk of magic hunting brought back all that former stress and led me to penetrate some of the mysteries that I experienced.'

'What was the blaze in the man's eyes and fingers? What do you think?'

'I couldn't say now. But then and there, as I lay prostrate in the midst of wild things, all my instincts alive and tense, I remember subconsciously feeling that the flame was the essence of the man's willpower exasperated by dire predicament, the sum total of the magic fluid collected and condensed from the person who was making the extraordinary effort to rout the danger.

'Without that magic force we should have been lost. Later I no longer thought of this, I forgot. But I now begin to understand again. As in the old hunters' magic, my man had grown and broadened out of himself, beyond his narrow wild nature, in order to take in and understand the wolf, assimilate him as it were. By thus magically knowing him could he subject and master him, in no other way. An enormous activity in spirit that we can no longer accomplish. The primeval magus was thus becoming the wolf's archetype, the great spiritual wolf beyond; before him the ordinary pack withdrew in fear, as men will at the sight of an angel. Prehistoric man did not hunt beasts, but chased dangers, shot his arrow at hostile mysterious forces, laid snares for purposes of existence.'

'You're exaggerating, your Honour,' a friend put in. 'I think that your man's blaze was common phosphorus, a rot such as produced by the wood of certain trees; he had soaked his hands and face ift it, to keep the beasts at bay. I have read this somewhere.'

'Quite possible, but the blazing was none the less magic,' the president agreed, quietly rubbing his ankle where the memory of pain, long ago experienced, was reviving.

THE NECROMANCER

Lawrence Flammenberg

When I had completed my time as a student I was appointed governor to the young Baron de R—, to conduct him on his travels. On our first journey we took our way through Italy, Switzerland, and Germany, and met, in this later place, with a most remarkable adventure.

Being arrived at the outskirts of the Black Forest, our postillion missed his way, as it began to grow dark, and at length did not know what direction he should take. Our fright was not little, when he apprised us of his distress, being desirous to get out of that dreadful forest as soon as possible, on account of the many instances of robberies and murders committed within its precincts, which the postillion had enlarged upon on the road; we therefore exhorted the fellow to go on, whatever might be the consequence. He did so, and after half an hour we came to an open spot.

'Now we are safe!' exclaimed the postillion joyfully, 'and, if I am not mistaken, not far from a village.'

He was right. We soon heard the welcome barking of dogs not far off, and a little while after we saw lights.

We entered a large village, but the inn was very different, and the landlord was amazed at the uncommon sight of gentlemen. His whole stock of eatables consisted of some smoked pud-dings, and a coarse sort of bread; he told us that neither wine nor beer could be got within the distance of many leagues and even our postillion could not drink his brandy. We asked him where the lord of the village resided; he answered that he never lived there, because the castle had not been habitable for many years. I enquired the reason of it.

'At present,' replied the host, 'I dare not give you an account of it, tomorrow you shall know everything; but, very likely, this night will make you guess the reason.'

The Baron and I entreated him to satisfy our curiosity, but he shook his head and left the room.

Pinched by hunger we took up with our scanty supper, and then asked the landlord to show us to our beds, but, alas! there was not one bed unoccupied in the whole house, and we were obliged to rest our weary limbs upon a bed of clean straw in the middle of the room.

The Baron soon began to snore, but I could not get a wink of sleep. Now the watchman announced the hour of midnight with a hoarse voice, and on a sudden I heard the trampling of horses and the sound of horns. The noise came nearer, and methought I heard a number of horsemen rushing by, and sounding their horns as if a large hunting party were passing through the village; the troop darted like lightning through the street close by the windows of the inn. The Baron started up, asking me with a fearful voice, 'What is this?' – 'I don't know,' replied I abruptly. I listened attentively, and the troop had not been far from our inn, when on a sudden all was again as silent as the grave; the Baron began to snore as before, and I to muse on that strange incident.

I could not think it possible that any body would go a hunting in so large a company, at that unseasonable hour, and was much inclined to think all had been a deluding dream, when I suddenly recollected the mysterious words of our landlord. I cannot but confess that I was seized with horror. I was just falling asleep when the voice of the watchman, crying one o'clock, roused me from my slumber. No sooner had he finished his round than the former noise was heard again at a small distance, I started up and ran to the window, but before I could open it the whole troop had rushed by like a hurricane. A little while after all was silent again, yet in vain did I beseech the god of slumber to take me in his arms.

The Baron had heard nothing the second time, snoring quietly by my side whilst I was ardently wishing for the morning, in order to satisfy my curiosity. I was too impatient to await the landlord's account of the castle, and when the watchman was crying two o'clock I hastened to the window, and began to converse with him.

'Watchman,' exclaimed I, 'what did that noise at twelve and one o'clock mean?' 'Your honour,' replied he, 'is certainly a stranger, for there's not a child in our village that does not know what that noise means; it is sometimes heard every night for several weeks, afterwards every thing is quiet again for a considerable time.'

'But,' said I, 'who is that person that goes a hunting at night?'

'That I can't tell you at present,' answered the watchman, 'ask your landlord, he will tell you all the particulars, I am here on my duty, and under the protection of Providence, but I dare not speak of what I hear and see.'

With these words he went away: – I wrapped myself up in my cloak, and sitting down by the window on a chair, expected, with anxious impatience, the rising of the sun. At length the eastern sky began to be embroidered with purple streaks, the crowing of the cocks sounded through the village, and the watchman announced the approach of day. The Baron awoke.

'You are very early,' said he, rubbing his eyes, 'pray tell me, what noise was it I heard in the night?'

'I myself am impatient to know it,' replied I, 'I wish the landlord would rise and unfold that mystery; the troop rushed by again at one o'clock with the same terrible noise.'

While I was talking thus, I heard the trampling of horses, and looking out of the window, saw an officer with a servant. They alighted at the inn, knocked at the door, and entered the room. The officer, a lively young man, wore a Danish uniform, and was on the recruiting business; he had missed his way like ourselves, and we soon got acquainted with him. When the Baron related the nightly adventure, the officer at first thought he was joking, but when I most seriously affirmed every circumstance, he showed an ardent desire to get acquainted with those nocturnal sportsmen.

'That honour you can easily have,' said the Baron, 'if you stay here the ensuing night, we will give you company.'

'Bravo!' exclaimed the officer, 'perhaps the gentlemen will be so polite to invite us to their sport, and then we may be so fortunate as to get a haunch of venison.'

Now the landlord entered the room. 'Well,' said he, bidding us a good morning, 'have you heard anything tonight, gentlemen?'

'More than I liked,' answered I: 'who are those sportsmen that go a hunting at midnight?'

'Why,' replied he, 'we don't talk of it: I would not tell you anything about it last night, for fear your curiosity might expose you to some misfortune; yet, having promised you yesterday to tell you as much of it as I know, I will be as good as my word.'

After having paused awhile, he began thus, in a confidential tone: 'Close by our village is a very large building, where formerly the Lord of this village used to reside. One of the former masters of the castle was a very wicked and irreligious man, who found great delight in tormenting the poor peasants; every body trembled when he appeared. He trampled with his feet upon his own children, confined them in dark dungeons, where they were often kept for many days without a morsel of bread. He used to call his tenants dogs, and to treat them as such – in short, he was cruelty itself.

'Hunting was his only amusement, and he always kept a vast number of deer, which were the ruin of the peasants' little property, and reduced them to the utmost poverty; no one dared to drive them from his fields, and if he did, he was confined in a damp dungeon, under ground, for many weeks. When that wicked man wanted to hunt, then the whole village was called together to serve him instead of dogs; if any one was not alert enough, then he would hunt him instead of the deer, till he fell down expiring under the lashes of his whip.

'One time after he had roved about from morning till night, he fell from his horse and broke his neck. He was buried in his garden. But now he was terribly punished for his wickedness, having had no rest in his grave to the present day. At certain times of the year he is doomed to appear in the village, at twelve o'clock at night, and to make his entry into the castle with his infernal crew, but as soon as the clock strikes one he is plunged back again into the lake of fire burning with brimstone. Nobody can inhabit the castle! Many who have been so fool-hardy to attempt it have lost their lives; whoever ventures to look out of the window when the infernal hosts are passing by gets a swollen face as a punishment for his curiosity. We are now used to that nocturnal sport, and do not care for those infernal spirits, but many strangers have fallen ill through fright.'

Here the landlord finished his tale, and seemed to be pleased with our astonishment; however, his pleasure was soon damped when the Lieutenant broke out in a roaring laughter.

'Laugh as long as you please,' said he; 'stay here till night if you have courage, and then we shall see if you will laugh.'

'That I will,' replied the officer, 'I will not only stay in your house, but I will also spend the coming night at that dreadful castle. I dare say, gentlemen,' added he, 'you will keep me company.'

The Baron, being a man of honour, thought it a great disgrace to betray the least want of courage in the presence of the soldier; he therefore promised to accompany him thither: I made several objections, representing to the officer the danger we should run, not knowing who those spirits might be; however, he silenced all my remonstrances: 'I am a soldier,' said he, 'and all ghosts and hobgoblins have ever been kept at a respectable distance by a martial dress.'

At length I was obliged to take a part in the expedition, if I would not desert the Baron. The landlord, who had all that time been staring at us in dumb amazement, lifted up his hands when I had consented to go to the castle, and entreated us, for God's sake, to desist from our undertaking: 'If you go,' added he, 'then all of you will be dead before tomorrow morning: for heaven's sake, dear gentlemen, do not run into the very mouth of the devil thus wantonly!'

However, the raillery of the Lieutenant put him soon so much out of temper, that he left us in great wrath, swearing in the height of his anger, that the devil would make us smart for our fool-hardiness and unbelief.

'Gentlemen,' began now the officer, 'pray let us take a walk to that terrible place, where we are going to spend the night, and reconnoitre it before dinner.' Approving of that proposal, we went all three to that residence of terror.

We approached and beheld the gothic remains of a half decayed castle, the gate was open and we entered the fabric. The arched walls, overgrown with moss and ivy, echoed to the sound of our footsteps; a long narrow passage led to a spacious courtyard, paved with stones; now we espied a spiral staircase of stone, and ascended it in dumb silence. A second long and narrow passage, which received a faint glimmering of light through several small windows, strongly guarded by iron bars, led us to a back door; the chilly damps of the long confined air rushed from the aperture when the Lieutenant had pushed it open; the apartment to which it led bore the gloomy appearance of a prison – the remains of half-decayed tapestry, covered with cobwebs, gave the room a dark dreary appearance; pieces of broken furniture were scattered about on the floor, a lamp hung in the middle from an iron chain fastened to the arched ceiling.

Just as we were going to leave this abode of gloom and horror, I perceived a little door in the remotest corner of the room, it was likewise unbolted, and we entered a second room, which bore the same gloomy aspect with the former apartment, being covered with half-rotten remains of broken furniture; another door led us at length into a spacious hall, where the cheering light of the day hailed us at last, many of the arched windows being either open or broken to pieces; the fresh air, the beautiful view meeting our eye from every side, chased at once from our countenance the solemn awe.

'Here,' exclaimed the Lieutenant, 'here we will meet the airy Lords of this Manor; Let us try, gentlemen, whether we cannot fit a table and some seats among the rotten relics of furniture.'

We succeeded in our attempt, dragged a round massy table in the middle of the hall, supported it by four worm-eaten poles, then we fetched some pieces of wood from the adjacent apartments, placing them upon large stones round the table, and thus secured a resting place for the night.

Now we rambled through several apartments on the other side of the hall, and meeting with nothing worthy of our notice, except the traces of desolation, we returned by the way we had entered that gloomy mansion.

We descended into the courtyard and made there likewise our observations: spurred on by curiosity, we entered through a ruinous side building, a garden, which still bore some marks of former grandeur; broken statues of marble were here and there lying on the ground. We cleared with our sabres a way through brambles and nettles to a grove of beech trees; it likewise was hardly penetrable.

Having worked our way for more than half an hour, with much toil and difficulty, through a thicket of thistles and brambles, we arrived at length wearied and fatigued at an open spot; in the middle of it we beheld a statue, bearing in one hand an urn of black marble – we approached and read the following inscription on the pdestal:

HIC JACET
GODOFREDUS HAUSSINGERUS,
PECCATOR.
(Here lieth Godfrey Haussinger, a Sinner.)
A little lower down we perceived a cross engraved in the stone, and under it

A.D. 1603.
We stared at each other in dumb amazement, and being already too much fatigued, we did not like to work our way farther into the garden, and returned.

'Gentlemen,' began the officer, as we were going back, 'what do you think of the inscription on that tomb?'

'I think,' replied I, 'it strongly corroborates what the landlord had told us.'

My companion smiled, and we came again into the courtyard, looking around we observed an arched wall opposite the staircase; as we came nearer we saw a flight of steps leading to a cellar, which was shut up by a massy iron door, strongly secured by an enormous padlock.

Having now examined every corner we returned to our inn.

The landlord, who was ignorant of what we had been about, was struck with horror and amazement when we related where we had been, and did his utmost to persuade us to desist from our design; however, when he saw he was spending his breath in vain, he kept his peace, and mentioned not a single word more about it during the whole day – we did the same – for the Lieutenant's conversation amused us so well, that evening stole upon us unawares.

Our dinner was better than our scanty supper on the preceding day, because the Lieutenant had brought with him an ample provision of ham and cold beef; some bottles of excellent wine, which he was also provided with, raised our spirits, and increased his and the Baron's courage, in such a manner, that they expected the approach of night with the greatest impatience – they were constantly looking at their watches, and as soon as the clock had struck nine, thought it high time to go to the castle.

We called the landlord to pay our bill, and the poor fellow tried once more to persuade us not to go to the castle: he entreated us not to expose our lives thus daringly to certain danger, and at last fell on his knees; – but when we left the room, without taking notice of his entreaties and ardent prayers, he lamented before hand our untimely death, gave us a lamp, and bolted the door, fetching a deep sigh.

The Lieutenant's servant walked before us, carrying the lighted lamp in his hand, and a portmanteau stocked with provisions under his arm, and we kept close to his heels, armed with sabres and pistols.

It was autumn, and of course very dark. We arrived at the castle; the faint glimmering of the lamp spread a kind of awful twilight around us as we were walking through the lofty arches of the vaulted passage leading to the courtyard. Having fired our pistols and loaded them again with bullets, we ascended the staircase; the doors leading to the hall we left open, that we might have a view of the courtyard, and sat cheerfully down to supper; a bottle of wine we had taken with us to keep us alert, was handed round: however, we missed our aim, for every one of us began to grow drowsy soon after we had finished our meal – we rose and walked about in order to avoid falling asleep, but we were soon tired of it, the ground being so very uneven, and returned to our seats. I recollected now, very fortunately, that I had put the fables of Gellert in my pocket. I took the book out, and began to read to the company; then I gave it to the Baron, and he was relieved by the Lieutenant – thus we were enabled to resist the powerful charms of sleep.

Now it struck eleven. All around us was buried in awful silence, which only now and then was interrupted by the creaking of our feeble chairs; the Lieutenant wound up his watch and put it before him on the table.

'One hour more,' began now the officer, 'and we shall be in another world.' Then he awoke his servant, who was fast asleep, and the Baron began again to read to us. – When the Lieutenant's turn came for the second time, he looked at his watch and exclaimed, 'three quarters past eleven, we must be on our guard.'

He got up and went to the window, I followed him, impenetrable darkness surrounded us, no star could be seen; awful silence was still all around, interrupted only by the snoring John, and the creaking of the wood; the pale light of our lamp produced a horrid glimmering in the spacious dreary hall; the Baron, leaning his head upon his arm, struggled to forget every object around him, and the officer uttered not a single word.

Now we heard a clock toll twelve at a great distance, and I walked softly back to my seat, the Lieutenant did the same, taking up one of his pistols, and rubbing the lock with his handkerchief. We looked at each other, and every one of us strove in vain to hide the horror he was struggling against. The watchman cried the hour, the crowing of the cocks told us midnight was set in, and still all round us was as silent as the grave. The Baron laid the book upon the table, and the Lieutenant was going to raise a loud laughter, asking us where the spirits might be, when suddenly the trampling of horses and the sound of horns was heard – we all were fixed to our seats, staring at each other with a ghastly look; now the noise seemed to be under our window; the Lieutenant ran towards it, with a cocked pistol in his hand, but he was too late.

All was quiet again, and an awful stillness swayed around the castle: however, a few seconds after we heard suddenly a most tremendous noise in the courtyard, which was followed by a terrible trampling and a jingling of spurs on the staircase, as if a great number of people in boots was coming up. The noise came nearer and nearer, my feet began to fail, my teeth to chatter in my mouth, and my hair to rise like bristles, while every sense was lost in anxious bodings; at length the noise grew fainter and fainter, and soon we could hear it no more, and midnight stillness resumed her awful sway.

A long pause of dumb astonishment ensued, until at last the

Lieutenant, who had recovered his spirits first, exclaimed, 'Shall we go down?' I shook my head without uttering a word, and the Baron was likewise silent. 'Then I will go alone,' said the Lieutenant, snatched up a brace of pistols, drew his sabre, and hurried down. He returned a few minutes after, exclaiming, 'It is surprising; I cannot see the least traces of either men or horses.'

Now he retook his seat, casting down his looks in a pensive manner – his servant was still snoring – the Baron began again to read, and I fell fast asleep. At once I was roused by the report of a pistol, I and honest John started up at the same moment, and we heard once more the trampling of horses and the sound of horns, but it soon died away at a distance, and the Lieutenant entered the hall with the Baron.

They also had not been able to resist the leaden wand of sleep, but the same noise in the courtyard we had heard at twelve o'clock had soon roused them from their slumber. 'As soon as we heard the noise,' said the Baron, 'we hastened to the outer room, our pistols cocked, but before we could reach it the noise was under the window of the castle; the Lieutenant knocked through one of the windows in the room close to the hall, and sent a bullet after the troop, which was rushing by like a hurricane; however, he was prevented by the darkness of the night from distinguishing anything except some white horses.

'The spirits are afraid of us,' exclaimed the Lieutenant now, 'but come, let us return to our inn, we shall rest more comfortable on a bed of clean straw than on this damp ground.' We all consented to it, and left the gloomy abode of those nocturnal sportsmen. We knocked a good while at the door of the inn before it was opened: and at last the landlord appeared, stammering, lost in wonder, 'God be praised that you are still alive, how did you escape?'

The Lieutenant silenced him by some hasty lies, and promised to give him a full account of the whole adventure after he should have rested a little.

'Gentlemen,' said he, as soon as he got up in the morning, 'next night I will go once more to the haunted castle, and spend the night in the courtyard, will you keep me company?'

The Baron looked at me if he wished me to refuse the proposal; I did so. 'We cannot,' said I, 'stay here a day longer, and such an undertaking would, besides, be too dangerous for only four people.'

'Oh!' exclaimed the Lieutenant, 'if that is all you have to say against it, then I will soon make you easy. We will take a dozen stout fellows from the village with us, they will not hesitate to accompany us if we give them a couple of dollars and a good dram; it will be devilish good fun, and tomorrow, with the first dawn of day, I will depart with you.'

The Baron consented to the proposal, and I myself did not dislike it; in short, we remained, and sent out postillion through the village to publish, 'that all young fellows who would go with us to the castle next night, should have sixpence each, and as much brandy as they could drink.'

In less than half an hour the whole village was assembled round the door of the inn. We selected fifteen of the stoutest, ordered them to provide themselves with proper arms, and to appear by ten o'clock at night at the inn. Our landlord, who beheld these preparations in dumb amazement, believed firmly that we must be arch necromancers, and his fancy having been fired by the wonderful account of our nocturnal adventure, which the Lieutenant had given him, he was himself not unwilling to go with us to the castle, and to bid defiance to the infernal hosts. However, as soon as it grew dark, his courage died away, and he wished success to our undertaking, telling us, he could not leave his house.

Our little army was assembled before ten o'clock, armed with scythes, poles, hay forks, and flails. We ordered the landlord to give a dram to every one: took some tables, benches, lamps, and a small cask of brandy with us, and marched in triumph towards the castle.

We pitched our camp in the courtyard, not far from the entrance, the peasants placed themselves round the brandy cask, lighted their pipes, and expected with pleasure the appearance of the airy gentlemen.

Another advantage we reaped from that honest company was, that we had no need to keep sleep at a distance by reading, for the merriment of our little army soon rose to the highest pitch, and these jovial fellows, being heated by the contents of our little cask, challenged his satanic majesty and all his infernal hosts amid peals of roaring laughter.

It was now past eleven o'clock, and the nose began to abate, some of our gentlemen were nodding, and some snoring, we were therefore obliged to beg those who had not yielded to the powerful charms of sleep, to give us a song, which they instantly did in so vociferous a manner, that our hearing organs were most painfully affected – the sleepers started up when they heard that terrible noise, and joined the jovial songsters with all their might. Thus we chased away the god of sleep, who seemed not in the least to relish the disharmonious notes of our jolly companions.

Now the Lieutenant beckoned to the blithesome crew, and the clamorous noise was suddenly hushed in awful silence. It struck twelve o'clock, and the sound of horns and the trampling of horses was heard at a distance. The peasants listened, their mouths wide open, and gazed at each other struck with chilly terror. No sound was heard, except the palpitating of their hearts, and here and there the chattering of teeth – all of them moved their lips as if praying ardently. The noise came nearer and nearer, and now it seemed to be in the castle. Again everything was silent, but in an instant the former noise struck once more our listening ears, and the infernal hosts rushed by like lightning – the Lieutenant, the Baron, and I darted through the passage leading to the gate, but the airy gentlemen were already out of sight, and we could see nothing, save a faint glimmering of some white horses. The mingled noise of their horns and of the trampling of their horses soon died away; the stillness of midnight swayed all around, and we returned to the courtyard.

Our valiant crew was still fixed to the ground, seized with horror and astonishment. None of them were able to distinguish whether we were ghosts or their fellow-adventurers; however, they recovered their spirits by degrees, and prepared to leave the residence of the infernal sportsmen.

We left the castle, fully convinced that these nocturnal ramblers must be being who were afraid of us, discharged our courageous troop and went to rest.

I awoke with the first ray of the morning sun, and roused the Baron and the Lieutenant; the latter seemed not to be inclined to fulfil his promise, being desirous to try his fortune once more, and to hide himself either in the courtyard, or before the gate. When he saw that we would stay not any longer, he postponed the execution of his design to a future time, and followed our example.

We left our inn at six o'clock, the morning was gloomy and rainy, the wind swept furiously over the heath, and drove the black clouds still closer and closer together; after a few minutes we entered the Black Forest. Looking out of the coach I saw the Lieutenant and his servant turn to the left towards a brook, where we beheld an odd incident. A reverend old man was sitting there, and reading in a large book; bewildered in profound meditation, he seemed to take no notice of the howling storm; and not to be sensible of the rain rushing down in large drops upon his uncovered head, the tempest was sporting with his reverend grey locks, and the rain beating in his face, yet he did not stir. His long brown robe seemed to denote a traveller from the East – a long staff and a black wallet were lying by his side.

I got out of the coach to view that strange being a little closer, and to speak to him, but before I could accost him, the Lieutenant exclaimed, 'Greybeard, what art thou reading?'

The old man appeared to take no notice of his question, and went on reading as if nobody had been there.

'What art thou reading?' exclaimed the Lieutenant once more, alighting and looking over his shoulder at the book.

The old man answered not a word, but still continued to read. I also was now standing behind him, and looking at the book, its leaves were of yellow parchment, the characters large and of different colours.

The Baron was close at my heels, and the Lieutenant being provoked by the man's obstinate silence, shook him now violently by the shoulder, thundering in his ears, 'Greybeard, what art thou reading?'

Now the old man lifted his reverend head slowly up, stared at us with angry looks, and then said, with a solemn awful voice,

'Wisdom!'

'What language is it?'

OLD MAN – (Reading again) – 'The language of wisdom.'

'What dost thou call wisdom?'

OLD MAN – 'All that thou dost not comprehend.'

LIUETENANT – 'If thou knowest what other people cannot comprehend, then I should like to ask thee a question.'

OLD MAN – (Staring again at him) – 'What question?'

LIEUTENANT – 'There is a castle not far from the next village, where every night a numerous troop of spirits make their entry; I and these two gentlemen have watched there these two nights.'

OLD MAN – (Interrupting him) – 'And art not a bit wiser for't, for thou seemest not to be fit to converse with spirits.'

LIEUTENANT – 'But thou – ?'

OLD MAN – 'I understand the language of Wisdom.'

The Lieutenant bit his lips, shaking his head with a contemptuous smile. Now the Baron accosted the old man, who again was immersed in profound meditation.

BARON – 'Well, then, if thy book contains such a treasure of wisdom, then tell us why that castle is haunted by spirits, and for what reason they go their nightly rounds?'

OLD MAN – 'That the spirits must tell thee themselves.'

BARON – 'What does then thy book contain?'

OLD MAN – 'The ways and means of forcing them to a confession.'

BARON – 'But why hast thou not forced them long ago to confess every thing?'

OLD MAN – 'Because I never cared for it.'

BARON – (Laughing) – 'But if we should entreat thee to do it, and pull our purses, would'st thou not do us that favour?'

OLD MAN – (Frowning) – 'Vile mortal, can wisdom be bought with gold and silver?'

BARON – 'How can one then purchase it?'

OLD MAN – 'With nothing – hast thou courage?'

BARON – 'Else we could not have watched in the dreadful castle.'

OLD MAN – 'Then spend another night in it. I will be there a quarter before twelve o'clock – now leave me.'

We gazed at each other with doubtful looks. The old man resumed his reading, and seemed to take no further notice of us, who were still standing behind him lost in silent wonder. At length the Lieutenant mounted his horse, and we went back to our coach. 'Well,' said the officer, as we were getting in our carriage, 'well, gentlemen, will you return with me?'

In vain did I make objections, the expectation of the two hot-headed young men was strained too much; it was impossible to subdue the eager curiosity of the young Baron, and the presence of the Lieutenant made me apprehend that all reasoning would not only be spent in vain, but at the same time make me contemptible; I therefore was forced to go back with them, and to embark in an enterprise, which, being not only useless, but also very dangerous, would plunge me in great distress.

Our host was highly rejoiced and struck with astonishment, when he saw us come back with the intention (as he believed) to engage once more with the nightly sportsmen. Our valiant companions of the preceding night had given a wonderful account of our adventure, relating how horribly the ghosts had looked, how courageously they had encountered the infernal crew, and how the strange conjurors at last had banished the tremendous host from the castle for ever.

The whole village assembled, therefore, as soon as our return was known, gazing at us as supernatural beings, and consulting us about several matters. The Lieutenant had his fun with the simplicity of those honest people and the day was spent merrily.

It was already dark, and the villagers had not yet left the inn; they unanimously entreated us to take them along with us to the castle. We were obliged to disavow our design, to feign sleepiness, and to order a bed of straw to be got ready.

At ten o'clock we stole silently to the castle without a light; the Lieutenant's servant lighted our lamp in the courtyard, and we went to the hall, where we had spent the first night, waiting with impatience for the last quarter before midnight. The Lieutenant did not believe the old man would be as good and his word; I joyfully seconded his opinion, and should have been glad if we had not waited for him; but the Baron, who, from his juvenile days, had been fond of every thing bearing the aspect of mysteriousness, was quite charmed with the reverend appearance of the old man, and maintained, upon his honour, that he certainly would stick to his appointment.

The Lieutenant began to discourse with the Baron on apparitions and necromancers, maintaining by experience and reasoning, that all was either deceit or the effects of a deluded fancy; yet the Baron would not relinquish his opinion, adding, that one ought not to speak lightly of those matters, and that the old man certainly would prove the truth of his assertion. We were still conjecturing who that strange wanderer might be, when we saw by our watches that there were but sixteen minutes wanting to twelve; as soon as it was three quarters after eleven we heard the sound of gentle steps in the passage.

'Our greybeard,' said the Lieutenant, 'is a man of honour,' and took up the lamp to meet the old man.

Now he entered the hall, his black wallet on his back, and beckoned in a solemn manner to follow him. We did so, and he led us through the apartments and the vaulted passage down stairs. We followed him through the courtyard to the iron gate of the cellar without uttering a word; there he stopped, turning towards us, and eyeing us awhile with a ghastly look; after an awful pause of expectation, he said with a low trembling voice, 'Don't utter a word as you value your lives.' Then he went down the two first steps; taking from his bosom an enormous key which had been suspended round his neck by an iron chain, and opened, without the least difficulty, the monstrous padlock, the door flew open, and the old man took the lamp from the Lieutenant, leading us down a large staircase of stone; we descended into a spacious cellar, vaulted with hewn stone, and beheld all around large iron doors, secured by strong padlocks; our hoary leader went slowly towards an iron folding door, opposite to the staircase, and opened it likewise with his key; it flew suddenly open, and we beheld with horror a black vault, which received a faint light from a lamp suspended to the ceiling by an old chain.

The old man entered, uncovered his reverend head, and we did the same, standing by his side in trembling expectation, awed by the solemnity that reigned around us; a dreaful chilliness seized us, we felt the grasp of the icy fangs of horror, being in a burying vault surrounded by rotten coffins. Skulls and mouldered bones rattled beneath our feet, the grisly phantom of death stared in our faces from every side, with a grim, ghastly aspect. In the centre of the vault we beheld a black marble coffin, supported by a pedestal of stone, over it was suspended to the ceiling a lamp spreading a dismal, dying glimmering around. The air was heavy and of a musty smell, we could hardly respire, the objects around seemed to be wrapped in a blue mist. The hollow sound of our footsteps reechoed through the dreary abode of horror as we walked closer.

The old man stopped at a small distance from the marble coffin, beckoning to us to come closer; we moved slowly on, and he made a sign not to advance farther than he could reach with extended arms. The Lieutenant placed himself at his right, I took my station at his left, and the Baron opposite to him.

He put the lamp on the ground before him, taking his book, an ebony wand, and a box of white plate out of his wallet. Out of the latter he strewed a reddish sand around him, drew a circle with his wand, and folded his hands across the breast, then he pronounced, amid terrible convulsions, some mysterious words, opened the book and began to read, whilst his face was distorted in a ghastly manner; his convulsions grew more horrible as he went on reading; all his limbs seemed to be contracted by a convulsive fit. His eyebrows shrunk up, his forehead was covered with wrinkles, and large drops of sweat were running down his cheeks – at once he threw down his book, gazing with a strange look, and his hands lifted up at the marble coffin.

We soon perceived that midnight had set in; the trampling of horses and the sound of horns was heard, the Necromancer did not move a limb, still staring at the coffin with a haggard look. Now the noise was on the staircase of the cellar and still he was motionless, his eyes being unmovingly directed towards the coffin. But now the noise was in the cellar, he brandished his wand and all around was buried in awful silence. He pronounced again three times an unintelligible word with a horrible thundering voice. A flash of lightning hissed suddenly through the dreary vault, lighting the damp walls, and a hollow clap of thunder roared through the subterraneous abode of chilly horror. The light in the lamp was now extinguished, silence and darkness swayed all around; soon after we heard a gentle rustling just before us, and a faint glimmer was spreading through the gloomy vault. It grew lighter and lighter, and we soon perceived rays of dazzling light shooting from the marble coffin, the lid of which began to rise higher and higher; at once the whole vault was illuminated, and a grisly human figure rose slow and awful from the coffin. The phantom, which was wrapped up in a shroud, bore a dying aspect, it trembled violently as it rose and emitted a hollow groan, looking around with chilly horror. Now the spectre descended from the pedestal, and moved with trembling steps and haggard looks towards the circle where we were standing.

'Who dares,' groaned it, in a faltering hollow accent; 'who dares to disturb the rest of the dead?'

'And who art thou?' replied our leader, with a threatening frowning aspect, 'who art thou, that thou darest to disturb the stillness of this castle, and the nocturnal slumber of those that inhabit its environs?'

The phantom shuddered back, groaning in a most lamentable accent, 'Not I, not I, my cursed husband disturbs the peace around and mine.'

OLD MAN – 'For what reason?'

GHOST – 'I was assassinated, and he who judges men has thrown my sins upon the murderer.'

OLD MAN – 'I comprehend thee, unhappy spirit, betake thyself again to rest; by my power, which every spirit dreads, he shall disturb thee no more – begone – '

The phantom bowed respectfully, staggered towards the pedestal, climbed up, got into the coffin, and disappeared; the lid sunk slowly down, and the light which had illuminated the dismal mansion of mortality died away by degrees. A flash of lightining hissed again through the vault, licking the damp walls, the hollow sound of thunder roared through the subterraneous abode of horror, the lamp began to again burn, and the awful silence of the grave swayed all around.

The old man took up his wallet and his book, beckoning us to follow him. We returned to the adjoining vault, through which we had entered that abode of awful dread; it was as lonesome as we had left it; our leader locked the iron folding-door carefully; then he took out his wallet a large piece of parchment on which a number of strange characters were written, a piece of black sealing wax, and a monstrous iron seal. Having made several crosses over these things with his ebony wand, he fixed the parchment above the lock, and sealed it hastily on the four corners.

This done, he went into the middle of the cellar assigning us our places; then he strewed sand on the ground, drew a circle with his wand, and began again to read in his book amid horrible convulsions. He brandished his wand, pronouncing three times with a most tremendous voice the same word he had made use of in the burying vault. A flash of lightning hissed through the cellar, a clap of thunder shook the subterraneous fabric, all the doors save that which had been sealed up were suddenly forced open with a thundering noise, the lamp was extinguished, and a blue light reflected in a grisly manner from the stairacse against the damp wall; woeful groans, lamentations, and the dismal clashing of chains resounded through the spacious caverns. The noise seemed to come from the staircase – gentle steps were heard – a numerous troop seemed to be descending into the cellar; the lamentations and the woeful groans advanced nearer, and louder resounded the clashing of chains.

Horrid to behold, did now a second phantom appear before our gazing looks, staggering slowly towards us, and leaving a numerous retinue on the staircase; the garment of the spectre was stained with blood, the skull fractured, the eyes like two portentous comets!

'Who art thou?' roared our leader with a thundering voice, and the dreary cavern echoed to the sound.

The phantom answered with a hollow, dismal voice, 'A damned soul!'

OLD MAN – 'What business hast thou in this castle?'

GHOST – 'I want to be redeemed from hell.'

OLD MAN – 'How canst thou be redeemed?'

GHOST – 'By the forgineness of my wife.'

OLD MAN – 'How darest thou claim it, reprobate villain? Return to thy damned companions in hell. Respect this seal, respect these characters.'

Here the old man pointed at the door of the vault which had been sealed up: the phantom staggered towards it, but suddenly shuddered back and sunk groaning on the ground; a flash of lightning illuminated the cellar, and a tremendous peal of thunder resounded through the lofty vault; all the doors were shut again with a terrible noise, a frightful howling filled our ears, and horrid phantoms hovered before our eyes; flashes of lightning hissed through the vault and roaring claps of thunder threatened to overturn the whole fabric.

The lightning ceased by degrees, and the roaring of the thunder died away, a blue flame was still glimmering on the staircase, but it soon died away, and we were surrounded with darkness; groans and dreadful lamentations resounded still through the winding caverns, but soon all around was hushed in profound silence. After a short pause of horrid stillness, the trampling of horses and the sound of horns was heard again; yet that noise died away also before we recovered our recollection.

When our astonishment began to subside, we perceived that we were standing in a dark cellar, without knowing whether any one of us was missing. A disagreeable sulphurous odour affected our smelling organs, and bereft us almost of the power of respiration; not a whisper interrupted the dead midnight silence which surrounded us. At length, somebody took me by the hand, I shuddered back, my imagination being still the wrestling place of horrid wild phantoms, and my soul divining a thousand dreadful thoughts.

'It is I,' said the Lieutenant, and I felt at once as if a heavy load had been taken from my breast. Now the Baron also began to speak, 'Where are you?' whispered he, 'are you still alive?'

We groped about in the dark, and at last found him leaning against the wall.

'How shall we get out of this cursed residence of horror?' exclaimed the Lieutenant. 'Come, let us try whether we can find the staircase. It must be just opposite to us, if I am not mistaken.' Then he began to walk on, and we groped after him, tumbling now and then over loose stones.

'I have found the staircase,' cried our fellow adventurer, 'at last, after a long fruitless search, I feel the first step.'

A ray of joy beamed through our hearts as we were climbing

up, but alas! it was soon most cruelly damped; the cellar door was locked up, and the blood congealed in our veins when the Lieutenant told it us. We exerted all our strength to force it open, but in vain, it was bolted on the outside. The Lieutenant called as loud as he could for his servant, whom he had left snoring in the hall; we joined our voices with his, calling with all our might, 'John! John!'

The hollow echo repeated in a tremendous accent, John! John! but no human footstep would gladden our desponding hearts. Frantic with black despair did we now begin to knock at the massy door till the blood was running down from our hands, and to cry John, John, till our voices grew hoarse – the hollow echo still repeated in an awful tremendous accent our knocking and crying, but no human footstep was heard. 'The fellow sleeps and cannot hear us,' said the Lieutenant, at length with a faint voice, 'let us sit down and watch him when he shall come down.'

We did so, but I had no hope that the servant would come, yet I concealed my apprehension within my breast. The Lieutenant dissembled to be easy, and began to converse on what we had seen and heard; however his broken accent, the faltering of his speech, and his low voice, betrayed the anxiety of his mind. The Baron and I spoke little, and when we had been sitting about an hour not one uttered a word more; all was silent around us. Nothing interrupted the death-like stillness of the night, except the violent beating of our hearts.

At length the Lieutenant asked if we were asleep; however, the anxiety of our minds and the dreadful apprehensions which assailed us, drove far away even the idea of sleep. We sat some hours in the dreadful situation, and it was now about five o'clock in the morning when the Lieutenant exclaimed, 'I fear we wait in vain for my servant, he cannot sleep so fast that he should not hear us! But where can he be?' Then he began again to knock violently against the massy iron door, but all was in vain. No human footsteps were heard, we remained some hours on the staircase, but all our waiting and listening was fruitless, no cheering sound of human footsteps would gladden our desponding hearts.

'I will not torment you by vain apprehensions,' began the Lieutenant at length, 'however, we seem to be doomed to destruction, yet let us try if we cannot escape some way or other, come down with me into the cellar, there we shall have a better chance to espy an outlet than here.'

We descended, with trembling knees, without saying a word, and groped along in the dark a good while, knocking our heads against the damp wall, and the iron doors. Alas! our search seemed to be in vain, and the grim spectre of a lingering death stared us grisly in the face, my feet could support me no longer, and I dropped down wearied with anxiety.

Now I began to reproach myself for having plunged into the gulph of destruction not only myself but also him who had been entrusted to my care. The apprehension of being famished in that infernal abode, thrilled my soul with horror and black despair; at first I heard the Baron and the Lieutenant still groping about; neither of them uttered a word; the hollow sound of their footsteps re-echoed horribly through the vault – at length the sound of the Baron's footsteps died away at a distance, and only one of my companions in destruction remained with me.

'Where are you?' exclaimed the Lieutenant.

'Here I am,' replied I, 'but where is the Baron?'

The Lieutenant called him, and I did the same, but we received no answer. At once a sudden hollow noise struck our ears, and at the same time a faint glimmering of light darted from a remote corner of our dungeon. I started up, half frantic with joy, and we pursued the gladdening ray of light; it seemed to come from an opening in the wall. No words can express the rapture we felt when we beheld one of the iron doors half open; we went through it with hasty steps, and entered a long vaulted passage. A faint dawn of light hailed our joyful looks at a great distance from below. We descended a declivity, the farther we went the more the light increased, at length we reached the end of the avenue, and perceived some steps leading into a spacious apartment, at the entrance of which some boards on the floor had given way. We descended the steps, and, who can paint the horror which rushed upon us, when we beheld the Baron lying lifeless in the deep vault, upon some mouldering straw? I leaped down without a moment's hesitation, the Lieutenant did the same, and now we began to shake the Baron till we at length perceived signs of returning life. We continued our endeavours to recall his senses, he breathed, gave a hollow groan, and opened his eyes: his fainting fit had been the effect of sudden terror, and he had not received the least hurt.

He now told us that he had met in the dark with a long narrow passage which he had pursued, in a kind of insensibility, till he had staggered down from an elevated spot, when the boards suddenly gave way, dragging him along into the deep vault.

Looking around we perceived that we were in a spacious cavern, which appeared to have been formerly a kind of stable. High over our heads were two large round holes, grated with strong iron bars, through which the daylight was admitted, and after a closer examination we espied a gloomy outlet in a remote corner, shut up by a wooden door, which we forced open without difficulty. We now ascended through a dark passage, higher and higher, till we at length with rapture beheld an outlet which opened into the garden; we were obliged to cut our way with our sabres, through the underwood and the entangled weeds, and soon came to the courtyard. Tears of joy sparkled in our eyes, rays of unspeakable rapture beamed through our hearts, and we praised God for our unexpected deliverance from the grisly jaws of a lingering death.

The dreary desolated courtyard appeared to us a paradise, the dazzling splendour of the bright morning sun, and the pure air which we now inhaled, filled our hearts with the strongest sensations of bliss. We congratulated each other on our resurrection from the dreary abode of mortality, where we were doomed to be entombed alive, and shook each other by the hand half frantic with joy.

We went now to the hall in search of the Lieutenant's servant; the table and everything was in the same condition we had left them, but John was not there. We went through the whole gloomy fabric shouting and hallooing, discharging our pistols, but no sound was heard except the hollow echo repeating our shouts and the reports of our pistols all over the dreary building.

'Very likely he is returned to the inn,' said the Lieutenant, 'and we shall find him there.'

We left that dangerous abode of black horror, praising God again and again for our deliverance.

As we entered the inn we beheld the landlord surrounded by a number of villagers, who were come to enquire whether we were returned from the castle. They were very much surprised when we entered the room, and, respectfully taking off their hats, told us, that the uproar at the village last night had been more tremendous than ever. Every one was impatient to know the particulars of our adventure, but the Lieutenant having then no inclination of amusing himself with their simplicity, gave them a short answer, and asked the landlord where his servant was.

'I have not seen him since yesterday,' replied he.

'It is impossible,' resumed the Lieutenant; 'where are the horses?'

'They are in the stable,' replied the landlord, 'I have just been looking after them.'

The Lieutenant gave us an apprehensive look, and begged the gaping peasants to look after him, all over the village and the adjacent places: they all were very willing to do it, and left the inn.

It was nine o'clock when we entered the inn, and it struck twelve when our honest villagers returned, with the disagreeable news that they could find poor John nowhere.

The Lieutenant thought it not prudent to remain any longer at that fatal place; the Baron likewise wished to depart and I too was impatient to be gone. As soon as we had finished our scanty dinner, we departed a second time; the tears started from the landlord's eyes, and from those of the good villagers, when we bade them farewell, after having made them a small present, and they saw us depart with regret.

The Lieutenant knew the ways through the Black Forest pretty well, he rode by our chaise leading his servant's horse with one hand, and we reached without any further accident the limits of that dreadful forest. We parted company at the close of the second day, bidding each other a tender adieu.

'I thank you, gentlemen,' said the Lieutenant, as we were getting into our chaise at the door of the inn. 'I thank you for your kind and faithful assistance in the most dreadful adventure of my life; if I should be so fortunate to get at the bottom of the mystery which hangs over that castle as I shall endeavour to do, I will take the first opportunity to appraise you of my success. Farewell, and do not forget your friend.'

At that the postillion smacked his whip and we went our different ways. On the fifth day we arrived, without any further incident, at the castle of Baron de R—, the father of my pupil. And here my narration ends.

Double Hex

SAMUEL M. CLAWSON

High summer in the Pennsylvania foothills often brings an oppressive humidity even in the coolest hours. It was already stuffy in the little bedroom under the eaves where Amanda Spiegell crouched in the light of a guttered candle, waiting for the dawn to make the cock crow. He was in a slatted box on the roof of the kitchen shed where he could see the low rise of Gobbler's hill to the east of Hummerstown.

She listened intently for any sound of her brother, Reuben, stirring in the second-floor bedroom directly beneath. If he guessed the cock was there, he'd surely know that she meant to strike at dawn when the tide of life is at full ebb, and he'd lay the cock still with his hex spell. The message in the tea leaves had been clear enough. A death in the family before the dark of the moon was done. There were only her and Reuben locked in the dark battle of hex and spell. The stark pattern in the bottom of the divining cup had warned her that the climax was at hand.

A faint greyness relieved the dead black at the window pane at the foot of her bed. The window was raised several inches at the bottom and the soft shuffle of spreading wings against the sides of the cage came to her ears. She crouched lower, bending over the floor. Her forefingers darted downward and inscribed an intricate sign as the cock began the first discordant notes of his call.

'Oh, brother, devil brother,' she spat out the words. 'Fade, pale, choke, smother, Fall, crawl, lie, die.'

A muffled snort from the bedroom below interrupted the last notes of the cock's crow. Amanda remained bent over, listening. She gasped with delight when a thumping crash shook the old structure of the house. Then, as she half rose from her cramped position, knife-like pain stabbed into her back.

The sound she made was an animal compound of surprise and

fury. She knew that somehow he had made a doll with a part of her in it. Not finger or toe clippings—she was careful about that. Perhaps a hair or two had escaped from the tight fitting house cap she always wore. There was nothing to be done now. Admitting receipt of a hex-blow only strengthened it tenfold. The knife-like pain had only been a cramp from bending over so long. She formed the thought as her defence, wishing grimly that she could believe it. Go down and fix his breakfast. Of course he carried the doll with him. No use looking for it. She had to crush him before he could use it again.

She pulled the stiff black skirt down over her ample hips, hurried into the blouse and tugged the comb through her iron-grey hair. Reuben's bedroom door was open when she came down the steps from the third floor and passed along the hallway. He had turned from the mirror and was watching when she stopped in the door. She remembered when she saw the costume. It was Wednesday morning. Every Wednesday morning he tried on the long scarlet cape and ugly white headthing with the black flap and eyeholes hanging over his face. She could see his piggy eyes shining behind the black cloth.

'Four eggs, Amanda,' he said thickly through the muffling cloth. 'And get rid of that damn rooster out there, wherever he came from—made me fall over the chair.' She could hear his voice in a diminishing mutter as she went on towards the steps. She felt the old creepy feeling on the nape of her neck and supposed that he was throwing his fateful hex-chant after her. 'Aiya, aiya, simple sister. Boil, burn, break, blister.' When he was alive father had never allowed it but Reuben had always found a time and place to whisper it in her ear.

It seemed years instead of six months since they'd put father in the ground. Reuben was the man and a woman has no say. He'd sold the farm and come to town. Rented a house and taken a job in Krause's butcher shop. Built the hex fire around her by day and by night—by chant and by spell. Oh, she knew the reason why. The money from the farm and what father had left in the bank. Reuben loved money. Every bite she ate was a piece of it—she'd seen it in his eyes.

The house was a spook's hold. He claimed to like it because the blind-alley street out in front ducked between Carter's warehouse and the City Garage to let out in the Main Square. He could whip around the corner and be at his job in Krause's Market in five minutes. Or to the Lodge on the other side of the square for an evening. After supper tonight he'd go up to his room, wrap the costume in a piece of butcher paper and go out to the lodge meeting.

She hated the house. Haunt-heavy and hex-walled. She thought of her Reuben doll, buried in the yard when it had failed her. The cat she had brought to set inside the seventh circle while she cast the death spell. He'd put the devil's horns on it with his thumb and two outside fingers. An hour later the cat had wandered out into the street in front of the house and Smeckler's grocery truck had ground the life out of him.

'Good eggs, Amanda,' Reuben looked up from his plate. 'Why don't you pull up a chair and have some?'

'You know I don't do that,' she said in a flat voice, turning from the stove and her puttering with the skillet. 'The men eat and then the women. Old custom is good enough for me.' She sniffed and went back to scraping at the bottom of the skillet. Why did he always think her a fool? He could put a sign on the egg in the shell or the flour in the bin and no matter. The fire would burn it out at cooking. He would get no chance to see her food between the cooking and the eating. Especially not now with the foot of the reaper already on the door sill.

'The trouble with you, Amanda, you're dumb as an ox.' Reuben sucked audibly at the cup of coffee and glanced at her back with a frown on his butcher's face. 'Hex is not for the likes of you so stop fooling with it. Some day you'll put the sign on yourself if you don't take care.'

'There's no money in the food jar,' she said coldly without looking around. 'Will you drop something in or bring some of Krause's horse flesh if you want to eat that.'

'We sell good meat.' He scowled at the thought of parting with money. 'Besides, I meant to tell you. We close the market for tomorrow. Krause and me are going rabbit hunting while they put the new counters in. Then you can make us a great big hassenpfeffer.'

After Reuben had gone she fried eggs and potatoes and sat at the table chewing nervously. Her eyes kept wandering to the wholesale meat company calendar on the far wall. She seldom noticed dates but yesterday she had traced the phases of the moon printed beside each day. In three more days—. She heard the front door open and turned to see Reuben standing by the clothes rack in the hallway.

'Damned rooster,' he said gruffly. 'Wondering how he got put up there on the roof and forgot my hat.'

She sat stiffly in the chair until the front door slammed then lifted a forkful of egg toward her mouth. Suddenly she drew in a harsh gasping breath. He'd seen the food. Of course the hex was on it. It must be that he too knew the time was near. Wily as a fox—he had almost trapped her. She snatched up the plate, car-. ried it to the garbage pail and scraped it off hastily.

When Amanda straightened up with the fork and plate still in her hand, her eyes were level with the calendar hanging slightly askew on the wall. Odd, she hadn't known this Wednesday was a red-letter holiday. Realization drenched her with the icy shock of startled fear. It was last month's sheet she was seeing. Her hand rose slowly and lifted the old sheet. The plate slipped from her other hand and shattered on the floor. No wonder he had come back. The new moon was due tonight. This was the day of the reaper forecast in the divining cup.

After the dishes were done she went upstairs to make the beds, her mind hunting wildly for a plan. When she pushed Reuben's door open her eyes went first to the table at the foot of the rumpled bed. It was a plain table with a lamp, an ashtray, and a rack of pipes. She had crocheted the large doily in the middle of the table. The hex sign was worked into it so cleverly that you could only see it by holding the doily up to the light. Sometimes he brushed the doily aside or left it carelessly tossed in the easy chair beside the table where he liked to sit and read. She always put it back to the sign of the devil's horns pointed up across the bed.

This morning the .22 rifle which usually hung on the wall above the bed was lying across the doily. The rifle was freshly oiled. The cleaning rod was leaning against the table and a box of cartridges spilled open beside the rifle. She looked along the barrel and saw that it pointed at Reuben's picture on the bureau. She came up to the table and reached out to lift the rifle. Then she saw that the doily was turned. She knew where the horns of the hex were by the little stitches she had dropped at the edge by each horn tip. The horns lay on each side of the rifle barrel and bracketed the picture on the bureau.

She drew her hand back without touching the rifle. It was a double sign. Strong hex and hard. She made the bed and hurried out of the room. For a while she sat in the kitchen, thinking, weighing, feeling more confident as she reviewed the lay of the hex. After a while she went back into his room and this time noticed that the rifle was loaded and the safety off. For a moment she frowned because this wasn't like Reuben. He was a careful one with a gun. Then she smiled. That was the way with hex. It changed little things—enough.

His dinner was hot in the pans when Reuben came in at five.

Instead of going to the stove and lifting the lids, he just stood there for a minute with his face the colour of a slab of suet. Then he went up the stairs. She heard him tramping around the bedroom like a caged animal. The he called down the stairs for her to come up.

'Get me a glass of schnapps,' he said gruffly when she came to the doorway. He was standing in front of the bureau and she could see his hands shaking all the way across the room.

'Just had a hell of an experience. Went over to Krause's house to look at his new gun. Picked the damn thing up and it went off Clipped through my hair. That close.'

Her mind raced while she went down the stairs and poured a glass on the pantry shelf. Oh yes, devil brother. One horn has missed you but the other is loaded too. Right there on the table. She listened unconsciously for the shattering report in the room above.

'Set it down. I'll get it in a minute,' he said when she came in with the glass. 'First, unload that damn gun, will you? I just noticed, it's loaded too.'

It was like a drench of cold water full in her face. How could both horns of a perfect hex have failed? She picked up the rifle and felt the weight of it in her hands. Almost as though by plan, her finger slipped inside the trigger guard and her hand clenched hard—like she had locked fingers uselessly around the neck of the Reuben doll. This time it was different. The rifle barked and ripped back in her hands. Reuben staggered one step and fell back on the bed.

She swayed forward with the rifle still clutched in her hands. In the ruin of his face where the bullet had found him, Amanda saw victory. She knew his spirit had lifted from him and her thought went flashing to the long knife-like splinter of yew-wood hidden in the bottom of her trunk. She'd saved a gallon of rooster blood to get it from old Granny Merk. Now, drive it through his heart and seal him out of the mortal world forever. She shook her head. It wouldn't do in this case with people coming and all. Anyway, he was the dumb ox—not her. Like mortal, like spirit—he'd never find his way back. She laid the rifle on the table and went down the stairs. A few minutes later she called the police.

It was an hour later and she was rocking back and forth in the old parlour rocker. The front door was open and the place was full of them. Dean, the plain clothes Chief, the coroner, two patrol car men in uniform, and a *Herald* reporter. As usual, Dean was talking.

'Damnedest thing I ever heard of. Picked up one gun over at Krause's place and shot a furrow through his hair. Then he comes home, picks up another, and bingo. You shouldn't have picked up the gun though, Miss Spiegell,' he frowned at Amanda. 'Besides disturbing the evidence, you mighta shot yourself. The rest of the clip was still in there.'

She looked up from her hands twisted together in the folds of the apron she was wearing and saw the flash of colour in the doorway. The squat figure wrapped in the long scarlet cape, the white hooded head, and the black face mask with the little piggy eyes shining behind it.

'Reuben,' her voice shrilled in the earache range. 'Oh damn you. I should have used the splinter.' She slid down into a moaning blubber.

One of the patrol men jerked his pistol from its holster and the masked man hastily pushed his hood back and showed his face. Everyone recognized Bill Stern, the shoe shop proprietor.

'What's going on here?' Stern asked plaintively. 'I just dropped over to ask about Reuben. Saw him sitting in his chair at the meeting. He was pale as a ghost and when I looked again, he'd

ANDREW LANG

Andrew Lang was born in Selkirk, Scotland in 1844. He attended the University of St. Andrews – which now holds the Andrew Lang lecture series in his honour – and Balliol College, Oxford, where he studied classical languages and literature. In 1875, Lang moved to London to pursue journalism. He became contributing editor of *Longman's Magazine*, and published widely in a number of other publications, including *Cornhill Magazine*, *MacMillan's*, *The Daily Post*, *Fortnightly Review*, *the Overland Mail*, *Fraser's* and *Time* magazine. He also wrote a good amount of fiction, much of it inspired by the folklore and myth of Scottish history. His *Fairy Book* series (1889-1910) remains popular to this day. Lang died in 1912, while living in Aberdeen, Scotland.

MATTHEW GREGORY LEWIS

Matthew Gregory Lewis was born in London in 1775. His father, a prominent public servant, intended for his son to have a diplomatic career, and Lewis was sent to Westminster School and then Christ Church College, Oxford. After summers spent in France and Germany – during which time he learned to speak German fluently and met Johann Wolfgang von Goethe – Lewis graduated in 1794, and became an attaché to the British embassy at The Hague.

While at university, under the encouragement of his mother, Lewis had completed two plays – *The East Indian* (1792) and *The Twins* (1794) – both of which were staged some years later. During his time in

The Hague, over the space of ten weeks, he produced *Ambrosio, or the Monk,* the work that would make him famous. A sensationalist, Gothic novel featuring ghosts, murders, and ravished maidens, the novel was an instant bestseller when it was published the next year. Henceforth known as "Monk", Lewis was a literary celebrity at the age of 20. In 1796, he began an indifferent six-year stint in the House of Commons, while continuing to write. In the years leading up to 1812, 18 of his dramas were published or produced at London theatres.

The death of Lewis' father in 1812 left him with a large inheritance, and in 1815 he sailed for the West Indies to visit his family's sugar plantations. He died at sea two years later, aged 42.

THOMAS PREST

Thomas Peckett Prest was born in 1810. Originally a talented musician and composer, Prest made a name for himself as a highly prolific producer of 'penny dreadfuls' – a Victorian era publishing trend of lurid and sensationalist stories printed over a series of weeks on cheap pulp paper. His most famous co-creation was the 'demon barber' Sweeney Todd, made famous by the story originally titled *The String of Pearls*. He is also thought to be the possible of author of *Varney the Vampire*. Prest died in 1859.

HECTOR HUGH MUNRO

Hector Hugh Munro was born in Akyab, Burma in 1870.He was raised by aunts in North Devon, England, before returning to Burma in his early twenties to join the Colonial Burmese Military Police.Later, Munro returned once more to England, where he embarked on his career as a journalist, becoming well-known for his satirical 'Alice in Westminster' political sketches, which appeared in the *Westminster Gazette.*Munro's first longer work, a historical treatise entitled *The Rise of the Russian Empire* appeared in 1900.His first collection of short stories, *Not-so-Stories,* was published two years later.After a stint as a foreign correspondent in the Balkans and Russia, Munro published *The Chronicles of Clovis* (1911), another collection of short stories which featured his most famous hero, Clovis.During World War I, he reached the rank of Lance Sergeant, and penned a number of short stories from the trenches.However, he was killed by a German sniper in November of 1916, aged 45.Arguably better-remembered by his pen name, 'Saki', Munro is now considered a master of the short story, with tales such as 'The Open Window' regarded as examples of the form at its finest.

FREDERICK MARRYAT

Frederick Marryat was born in Westminster, London in 1792. After trying to run away to sea several times, he was permitted to enter the Royal Navy in 1806, and spent the following 24 years serving on a variety of frigates, travelling to places as far-flung as Burma and Bermuda and eventually rising to the rank of captain. In 1829, he published his first novel, *The Naval Officer,* and resigned his naval commission a year later in order to take up writing full-time.

From 1832 to 1835, Marryat edited *The Metropolitan Magazine.* He kept producing novels at a rate of almost one per year, with his biggest success, *Mr Midshipman Easy*, coming in 1836. He moved to London in 1839, where he was in the literary circle of Charles Dickens and others. In 1843, not long after being named a Fellow of the Royal Society, Marryat moved to a small form in Norfolk, from where continued to pen novels. Some of these, such as *The Children of the New Forest* (1847), were aimed at children, and were well-received by contemporary audiences.

Marryat died in 1848, aged 56. He is seen now as one of the pioneers of the sea novel, and acknowledged as a major influence on writers such as Joseph Conrad and Ernest Hemingway.

VASILE VOICULESCU

Vasile Voiculescu was born in Pârscov, Romania in 1884. In 1902, after finishing his basic schooling, he read philosophy for a year at the University of Bucharest, before switching to medicine. He qualified as a doctor 1910, and began to write shortly afterwards.Voiculescu's literary debut came in 1912,with the publication of his poem 'Dor' ('Longing').In 1916, he managed to publish a volume of poetry, but the German forces occupying Bucharest destroyed all copies. Between the two World Wars,Voiculescu managed to publish a good deal of poetry, as well as a number of short stories, novels and plays. He died in prison, having been incarcerated by the post-War Romanian authorities for publishing non-Communist sentiments.In 1990, he was posthumously elected a member of the Romanian Academy.

LAWRENCE FLAMMENBERG

Lawrence Flammenberg was the pseudonym of German author Karl Friedrich Kahlert, born in 1765. Very little is known about his life, and he is primarily remembered for his Gothic novel, *The Necromancer; or, The Tale of the Black Forest,* first published in 1794. Consisting of a series of lurid tales of hauntings, violence and the supernatural, all set in Germany's Black Forest and featuring the resurrected wizard Volkert the Necromancer, *The Necromancer* is one of the seven 'horrid novels' lampooned by Jane Austen in *Northanger Abbey.* For a considerable amount of time, Kahlert's tale was thought not to exist except within the text of Austen's novel. Kahlert died in 1813.

www.ingramcontent.com/pod-product-compliance
Lightning Source LLC
Chambersburg PA
CBHW030344030726
47499CB00003B/886